Bliss Adair

AND THE FIRST RULE OF KNITTING

JEAN MILLS

Red Deer Press

Published in Canada by Red Deer Press,
209 Wicksteed Avenue, Unit 51, Toronto, ON   M4G 0B1.

Published in the United States by Red Deer Press,
60 Leo M Birmingham Pkwy, Ste 107, Brighton, MA 02135.

Red Deer Press acknowledges with thanks the Canada Council for the Arts
and the Ontario Arts Council for their support of our publishing program.
We acknowledge the financial support of the Government of Canada through
the Canada Book Fund (CBF) for our publishing activities.

 ONTARIO ARTS COUNCIL
CONSEIL DES ARTS DE L'ONTARIO
an Ontario government agency
un organisme du gouvernement de l'Ontario

 Canada Council   Conseil des arts
for the Arts   du Canada

Library and Archives Canada Cataloguing in Publication
Title: Bliss Adair and the first rule of knitting / Jean Mills.
Names: Mills, Jean, 1955- author.
Identifiers: Canadiana 20230419426 | ISBN 9780889956841 (softcover)
Classification: LCC PS8576.I5654 B55 2023 | DDC jC813/.54—dc23

Publisher Cataloging-in-Publication Data (U.S.)
Names: Mills, Jean, 1955-, author.
Title: Bliss Adair and the First Rule of Knitting / Jean Mills.
Description: Toronto, Ontario : Red Deer Press, 2023. | Summary: "Bliss Adair, 16, ace
knitter and math whiz, discovers that some secrets are meant to share while others are not. Her
involvement in the dilemmas of friends is well intentioned – but is that enough? And does the first
rule of knitting – don't look too far ahead – always apply to life?" -- Provided by publisher.
Identifiers: ISBN 978-0-88995-684-1 (paperback)
Subjects: LCSH: Teenage girls – Conduct of life -- Juvenile fiction. | Knitters (Persons) --
Juvenile fiction. | Social skills -- Juvenile fiction. | Friendship in youth -- Juvenile fiction. |
BISAC: YOUNG ADULT FICTION / Coming of Age.
Classification: LCC PZ7.M555Bl | DDC 813.6 - dc23

Edited for the Press by Beverley Brenna
Text and cover design by Tanya Montini
Printed in Canada

www.reddeerpress.com

In memory of my mother, Ruth Bangay. She showed me how to knit. She also showed me how to help—by listening.

1. OVERHEARD

She obviously doesn't know I'm curled up on the window seat just behind the curtain or she wouldn't have come down the dark hallway and stood outside the bathroom and told whoever was on the other end of the phone that she was having an incredible time with him but he's almost as young as Finn and it's just so weird.

Several things occur to me.

First, she must have been the latecomer, the "Oh, hi, you must be Lauren" my mom welcomed to tonight's Knit & Natter, because I had already met all the other attendees, before retreating down the hallway with my Alpaca Merino Chunky and size 6mm's.

Second, she doesn't sound like a kid. She sounds like my mom. Well, not what she's saying, of course, but her voice. It's a mom-age voice. Sure, I know moms can be quite young. Still ...

7

Third. I actually know a boy named Finn. He's a guy at school. He's in my math class, very smart. Plays on the basketball team. Has a girlfriend named Karlee. Different crowd—well, I don't really have a crowd—but yes, Finn Nordin.

Here are the questions I ask myself:

Is Lauren the mother of Finn from my math class?

And is she having a hot romance with some high-school guy? University guy, maybe?

I wait, frozen. I don't want her to hear my needles clicking, peer around the corner of the hallway and find me curled up in the shadows on the window seat, with my knitting and my big ears, and an expression on my face that says: "Eew. Yes, I heard you."

"Honestly, it's the most fun I've had in years," Lauren is whisper-laughing into the phone. "I feel like a teenager." Pause. Age-inappropriate giggle. "I know, eh?"

Crap. I wish she'd shut up or continue this call in the bathroom, behind a locked door. Maybe I *should* make a noise ...

A big laugh from the front of the store, and my mom says: "Oh, Oscar!"

Finn's mom is now whispering into the phone.

"I should go. I'm at this knitting thing. Told Dan I was joining so he wouldn't start asking questions about me going out at night." Pause. "I know, eh? Absolutely high school confidential. Am I crazy? Yes, I'm crazy. Gotta go. Byeee!"

She giggles, and then I hear her heading back down the hallway and laughing as she joins the group in the front room: "What did I miss?"

I just stay here on the window seat and return to my knitting—so soothing, so rhythmic, so orderly—wishing I hadn't heard what I just heard.

2. ANDERSON

Anderson drops into the seat across from me in the cafeteria, peels off his backpack and drops it on the floor, leans forward onto his folded arms, and grins at me.

Hmm. Odd. Anderson is not a grinner. He is a smiler, a hugger, a belly-laugher (and he has the belly to go with it. Not an insult. A truth, long acknowledged by all of us). Grinning is not usually in his social repertoire.

"What?"

He just grins some more. Gives a little crack of his head to the side. He's trying to tell me something ...

"You didn't," I breathe.

"I did. You told me to, and I did it. Signed up for volleyball tryouts."

I can't help the huge smile that splits my face open, and makes my voice go up two octaves. "You did? Really?"

"Yes, I did. And if it's a catastrophe, I'll blame you."

We high-five. "Fair," I say.

The thing is, Anderson has volleyball in his genes. His grandfather went to the Olympics on the Bulgarian (... I think ... maybe Hungarian?) volleyball team in some distant competitive past, and his mom was a star at university, apparently. I've seen him set a volleyball into the air with fingers so strong, you don't even hear the ball, just a soft *pfft* as it lifts back up, ready to be smashed. And for someone so big—okay, let's just say enormous— he moves like a cloud in the sky, all smooth and light.

The problem is that he doesn't fit the classic athlete look, so no one takes him seriously when he shows up in his baggy size Triple-X Large shorts and T-shirt. In elementary school, in middle school, with kids we'd known since kindergarten, well, that was okay. But here in the big leagues of Central High School, with kids from all different neighbourhoods, he just never wanted to put himself out there.

"I'm proud of you," I say, and he shrugs.

"I told the Gang of Five in gym class, and they were suitably impressed," he says, reaching for his lunch bag.

Ah, the Gang of Five. The name Anderson and I have given the boys from our grade who are on all the teams, who hang out together at school and out there in the real world—who we've known since kindergarten.

Okay, they're not that bad, but they can also be bad. Especially to Anderson, in that sneaky known-you-forever, no-secrets, hey-buddy-just-kidding kind of way. Of course they know and accept that Anderson is gay. They are not dangerous, that way. Just, I don't know, just annoying.

John Bryant, Peter Abella, Preston Glavin, Vic Tran, and Cameron Tellez.

"What did they say?"

"Actually, Peter impressed me," grins Anderson, taking a huge bite of his drippy pita sandwich and leaving a huge smear of mayonnaise across his upper lip. "He told me, 'Fat chance, Varga.' I thought that was rather good." He chews and grins.

"Screw the Gang of Five," I say and grin back at him.

Cameron Tellez, member of the Gang of Five, appears at the end of our table, carrying a tray with today's offering of some kind of mystery pasta and a large chocolate milk. He looks at Anderson and opens his mouth as if he's going to say something, but before he can, one of the other jerks shows up and pretends to run into him, and there's a stupid moment of jerk-laughing and they move off.

Anderson ignores it. Or maybe he just didn't see.

Me, I see everything.

3. MATH CLASS

That guy Finn—the one whose mother I think might be having an embarrassing romance with a guy not much older than he is—that Finn—just walked through the door of the classroom, and briefly locked eyes with me.

He didn't really see me, though. His glance just happened to land on my coordinates—the middle of the middle row, which I like to think of as the intersection of the x and y axis—and flit away, back to his buddy, Dev, and a girl. Not Karlee the girlfriend, but another girl he hangs out with, Adele.

Close call. I don't really want to talk to him or anything. ("Hey, is your mom named Lauren? Did you know she's having an affair with some young guy?") No, no, none of that. I don't even want to draw his attention.

I'm just curious. I mean, how many guys named Finn are there in our neighbourhood?

"Are you into Finn Nordin?" Bethany leans over and whispers, trying to hold my eyes.

So, my move was observed after all.

"No," I shrug her off. "Who?"

"He has a girlfriend," she says. "Besides ..."

"All right, everyone, you'll need paper and pencil for this one," Mr. Wenzik interrupts, still at the whiteboard, writing what looks to be a quadratic equation problem. "Close those laptops. Textbooks not needed."

I glance at Bethany, eyebrows raised. "Besides?" but she has already turned away and is opening her binder, ready for the class.

Besides?

She might be referring to that now-embarrassing comment I made, once, during the second week of school, when I admired the way Taz Fenwick looked in his gym uniform. A passing comment on the perfection of his proportions—legs, waist, shoulders, arms. Like a Ken doll from that old suitcase of ancient Barbies my mom hauled out for us when we were in kindergarten. Proportions work for me. It wasn't about Taz, the boy, at all, but Bethany being Bethany ... maybe that's the *Besides?*

Sometimes I just can't keep up with people. Either that, or they can't keep up with me. Maybe that's it. I've known Bethany forever, but sometimes we are mysteries to each other.

"Quadratic equations, people." Mr. Wenzik cuts my thoughts into shards and scatters them. Thank goodness.

Give me math over boys any day. Even perfectly proportioned boys like Taz Fenwick. Boys actually scare me a little. Okay, not in a creepy #MeToo way. Just the whole dating, hand-holding, kissing thing. And what comes next. All the stuff that Bethany likes to go on about—the romance movies, the books she reads. Math and knitting are so much easier to deal with because they are problems that can be solved, using a precise process, following steps that form patterns. Unpredictable, maybe, but with a clear solution, even when viewed through the lens of my mother's First Rule of Knitting: Don't look too far ahead.

So, yeah, Taz Fenwick is perfectly proportioned, but I look no further than that.

I snap back to the classroom as Wenzik turns around, after writing something on the board.

"Here is a quadratic equation," he announces, pointing. Ah. My happy place. "Solve it, using the process we followed last class. I want to see your proof. Yes, you may work with a partner," he adds as hands go up. For some reason, my classmates are heavily into working with partners.

So, Bethany and I move our desks together—everyone is doing the same thing. Much thumping and screeching of metal legs on the floor.

"Okay," she says. Bethany likes to take control of any group situation, and I'm happy to let her. "Find the root of $x^2 - 14x + 46 = 0$," she reads off the board. "Oh crap. I don't even remember where to start."

I do, though. I write the question down and take a moment to let it all grind together, then:

"The answer's 7 plus or minus the square root of 3."

Bethany puts her head down on the desk and whines. "I knew you were going to do that."

Mr. Wenzik has been watching, of course. He walks slowly up the aisle until he's standing in front of our desks.

"Trouble here, Bethany?"

"Um, no, Mr. Wenzik."

He looks at me. That look. "Bliss?"

Oh-oh. I did it again.

"Um, yeah, the answer's 7 plus or minus the square root of 3." I keep my eyes on the paper.

"And showing your solution? Remember that part?"

"Oh, right."

I pick up my pencil and quickly write:

$x^2 - 14x + 49 - 3 = 0$

$(x - 7)^2 - 3 = 0$

$(x - 7)^2 = 3$

$x - 7 = +/- \sqrt{3}$

$x = 7 +/- \sqrt{3}$

I look up at him then and realize that the classroom is now silent. Everyone has been listening, because I spoke the solution out loud as I wrote it, figure by figure, line by line.

"Sorry," I mouth to Bethany, who is just shaking her head.

We have all been here before. I can't help it if I see math problems laid out in perfect, precise, easily managed lines and patterns, can I? No, I can't.

"I just see it," I weep, trying to explain to my Grade 3 teacher when I got yelled at for, once again, calling out the answers in math class, before any of my classmates even had a chance to pick up their pencils.

"It's a gift," says my dad. "It's what makes you so good at creating original and very cool knitting patterns."

I just see it. Numbers. Lines. Stitches. Patterns. The "what next" just seems to appear in my head, clear and real.

"And why 49?" asks Mr. Wenzik.

"Because this, the left side," I point at the original question with my pencil, "is close to being factorable by $x - 7$, so I changed the constant term into two parts."

I look up at him and take a quick look around.

Everyone is looking back at me. For a second, my eyes meet Finn's, and, astonishingly, he grins at me.

I quickly look away.

"Well, you're right again, Bliss," says Mr. Wenzik. He sighs, shakes his head, then smiles at me and turns around to go back to the board. "And since everyone heard that solution, we'll just go through it together up here on the board, and then I'm giving you another problem."

He looks over his shoulder at me. "And Bliss, you'll write the solution silently this time, right? And pull the plug on calling out the answer?"

"Yes, of course. Sorry, Mr. Wenzik."

"No need to apologize. That was very helpful. Now, let's see." He's at the board, marker hovering, as he prepares to take the class through the proof.

I glance over my shoulder at Finn again, but he's already watching Mr. Wenzik. Adele sees me looking, though, before I turn back to the front.

4. THE FIRST RULE OF KNITTING

My parents named me Bliss because, says my mom, I was the most blissful gift she was ever given.

I know. Cheesy.

But it could have been worse. Apparently, while waiting for my arrival, the girl's name they had chosen was Guinevere Avalon. Yes, Guinevere Avalon Adair. Can you even imagine how cruel that would be? (If I had been a boy, their first choice was Lancelot Arthur. Still unusual, but at least workable.)

Someone talked them out of it. Thank you, Auntie Bryn, who said names from Arthurian romance are fine, but "that *Guinevere* part. Oh, my God, think of the child, please, Rowan."

"Fine. Then we're going with our second choice."

"Oh, dear." Auntie Bryn is said to have covered her face in her hands and replied, "Hit me."

"Bliss."

"But that's a lovely name," Auntie Bryn said, apparently. "For which? A boy or a girl?"

"Yup, exactly. Boy or girl," my dad said. "Perfect happiness. Great joy. Bliss Carman."

Sometimes he hauls his grandfather's old poetry anthology off the shelf and turns the yellowed pages until he comes to this beauty that begins: *O all the little rivers that run to Hudson's Bay, They call me and call me to follow them away.* Bliss Carman, some random Canadian poet of the early twentieth century, and one of my great-grandfather's faves.

So, whether I was named for some old poet, or because I represent perfect happiness and great joy, I don't really know.

I just know that my parents are different from many of my friends' parents for all sorts of reasons, and I like it.

First, they were old when they had me. I arrived like magic, my mother says, after years of "trying" (eew, I prefer not to think about this). And they were in their early forties, convinced that they would never have children, and perfectly happy about it, actually.

Dad was head of sales and marketing at a giant and well-known chain of craft stores. Mom was teaching fibre art techniques at a downtown Toronto university. They had jobs, took fun trips (camping in Australia, hiking in Iceland, cruises to Antarctica and around Norwegian fjords), volunteered, donated to good causes, hung out with friends playing guitars.

And then Mom started feeling sick in the mornings, and the next thing you know ...

Me.

"You should never look too far ahead in Life," she always says. "You just never know."

Mom and I are alone in the store this afternoon.

She's on the computer, going through orders. I'm at the table in the front window, knitting a shawl. It's a new pattern I'm playing with, but I'm not sure. This alpaca fleece is wonderful to work with, but I think it might be wrong here. Maybe a little too "buttery," as we yarn nerds call it. Also, I might be overdoing it on the bobbles and shells. Too many textures. I'm tempted to rip it out and start over with more of a herringbone. Or go wild with some eyelet and lace, although, with this chunky yarn—maybe just fewer bobbles ...

Absolutely high school confidential. Am I crazy? Yes, I'm crazy.

Usually, the stitches and pattern unfold slowly and methodically in my head, almost talking to me, before they fall under my fingers. Usually.

The problem is, today, in my head, I keep hearing Lauren-who-might-be-Finn's-mother whispering in the hallway. It's so annoying. Especially since I now find myself trolling this poor guy at school, wondering if he has a socially irresponsible parent. That glance in math class. Later this afternoon in the hallway, when we passed going in opposite directions, he didn't even look at me, and I'm pretty sure I'd turned back to Bethany before Adele and Karlee noticed.

This guy and his mother (but *is* she his mother?) are complications. I do not need complications in Life. Just in math problems and knitting patterns.

"Whatever are you glaring at?"

Back to the table by the window and my buttery alpaca fleece and the pattern that isn't working. I look up at my mother and shrug.

"Don't think this pattern is working." I hold up my needles and the ten inches or so of blue heathery yarn that was supposed to be the start of an unusually textured shawl. "I think it's time to rip it out and start over."

"Or you could keep going," she says, eyes back on her computer screen.

My mother taught me to knit when I was old enough to hold the needles and sit still. I was five. She was forty-eight and the new owner of String Theory, this little shop on a downtown side street of our small community, just west of Toronto. She and my dad had quit their jobs, sold the big-city house, and changed everything.

"That's what having a kid will do to you," Dad explains,

whenever he tells the story of how many people tried to talk them out of it. "You just never know what's coming."

With their combined savvy in sales, marketing, and fibre art, they were an instant commercial success. They bought an old house, fixed it up, and threw themselves into being my parents, running their little downtown store, and enjoying a slower pace of life.

"If anyone had told me..." Mom always says. She never finishes the sentence, just raises her hands in a giant shrug and laughs.

So, at age five, there I am, sitting with her at the table in the window at String Theory after my day at kindergarten. I can still see it—Dad at the counter with the computer, a few customers coming by, chatting, saying, "Oh, isn't that just the cutest thing!" as Mom hands me the short, fat, kid-friendly needles with ten cast-on stitches in a bright blue yarn, a soft and shiny yarn that I chose myself.

"See? Like this."

She demonstrates how to hold the needles, pick up the loop of the stitch, swing the yarn over, slide the needle around and through, and drop it into place. I copy the motions and knit a stitch on mine. Look up at her, and she nods, smiling. She knits another stitch, I knit another stitch. We're knitting together.

It's an orderly process that follows a predictable pattern, so I already love it.

Two more stitches. I might be smiling now. Mom is laughing and Dad is cheering me on from the counter.

"You're a natural, Bliss. Of course you are!"

But something worries me about this—

"But wait, Mom. Wait. What happens when you get to the end of the loops?"

She sets her needles on her lap and leans toward me, so our faces are close together.

"Oh, Bliss," she whispers. "Trust you to think of that, because *that* is the big question."

"It is?" I am already, at age five, into big questions. Questions about numbers, about the difference between the white and black keys on the piano, about the speed of the clouds, about the lines on the measuring cup we use to make muffins.

"The First Rule of Knitting," my mother whispers, "is not to look too far ahead."

So now, here I am, eleven years later, with a knitting pattern on my needles that I don't think will turn out right, and an annoying woman in my head, who may or may not be about to complicate the life of a boy I don't know very well. Rip it out? Care? Or just be quiet and keep going?

"I guess I'll just keep going," I say to Mom. "See what happens."

"Good girl," she smiles, eyes still on her computer. She has no idea what I'm really talking about.

5. THE PREGNANT GIRL

On the way to homeroom on Monday morning, I see her standing in the hallway with Mrs. DiLello, school principal, and our homeroom-also-English teacher, Ms. George. Papers, maybe a timetable. A school-issued daily planner (a very old-school tradition, but I'm okay with it. I actually use mine). Conversation of an administrative nature is obviously underway.

Sydney Bart. It has to be.

As I slip by into the classroom, our eyes meet and I smile at her, quickly.

Nothing. Then, a moment after she has turned her head to listen to something Mrs. DiLello is saying, a quick glance back at me, a nod. A weak smile. More of a twitch.

Yes, the String Theory communications network has done its work.

The store was super busy last Saturday afternoon, so it was a good thing all three of us were there on duty.

Mom is helping people find things and indulging her yarn-girl passions. ("You will *love* this new sock yarn, Marianne!" "Oh, thanks, Rowan. I haven't even heard of this one." "Just got it in. Hand-dyed at a little farm up near Mount Forest. Met the farmer at One Of A Kind in November and was just smitten with it.") I can't see them—they're somewhere up the fingering-yarn aisle—but I can picture them. Hands on the skein, squeezing, grinning, squeezing some more, feeling the imaginary sock (or shawl, or whatever) knitting itself into existence.

Dad is on cash and he's busy. For some reason, the lead-up to (still distant) Christmas season and the approach of winter sends all the knitters into a frenzy, and they suddenly have to top up their yarn stash, replace needle sets, find some new project to launch. Socks are big. Baby blankets and afghans. We've been selling a lot of specialty yarn for crocheting tiny creatures, like unicorns, owls, and dinosaurs. We just sold $200 worth of textured black, red, and white worsted to a woman who is planning to corner-to-corner crochet the logo of the Toronto Raptors into a bedspread for her basketball-obsessed son.

"Oh, wow," says Dad, impressed. "I'd better start stocking NHL colours, too. Get Bliss working on some pattern charts for those logos. Great idea, Ann. Thanks!"

Between them, my parents know everyone who comes in. If a new customer arrives, my parents know everything about them before New Customer leaves. Name, where they're from, knit or crochet, preferred projects/colours. People comment on it, laugh, a little bit in awe, I think.

"String Theory," says Dad. "We try to be the furthest thing from theoretical."

He thinks he's funny. People laugh, so maybe he is. But when it's your own dad, well ...

While they're looking after the commercial side of things, I'm at the table by the window, in charge of the drop-in Help Desk. (Yes, Help Desk. Just like in the IT department of some big company, which is, of course, where Dad got the idea.)

"I dropped a stitch way back here. Can you help?" Yes, I can.

"I don't understand these instructions in the pattern—*yfwd* and *tfl*. Can you show me?" Yes. Yes, I can.

"I have a feeling I goofed." Yes, you most certainly did.

"Can you do me a favour, Bliss?"

The Help Desk has actually been a bit quiet today, so I've been head down, digging into some intense German short rows on a project Mom started and asked me to work on for a sweater display she's planning: *knit to the marker, slip the marker, knit one, turn the work, wrap the stitch, knit to the marker, slip the marker, close the gap, knit to the stitch past the gap, turn the work, wrap the stitch* ... Not paying much attention, so she takes me by surprise.

Mrs. Bart, one of our senior customers, knitter extraordinaire.

"Of course, Mrs. Bart," I say, noticing right away that she doesn't have a project with her. In fact, I can't imagine there's any knitting situation that I could possibly help her with. She could be running the Help Desk herself. "Um, a knitting favour?"

"No, no, not knitting, dear."

She sits down next to me. Plunks herself down, as if her legs are tired. Sighs.

I hate it when grownups sigh. When they look at you the way Mrs. Bart is looking at me right now. Clearly, all is not right in her world, and it worries me that she thinks a favour from a sixteen-year-old high-school student could help.

"What can I do to help?" I ask, of course.

"It's—well, it's a bit delicate, so I'll just come out with it."

For a terrible moment, I'm sure she's going to say she knows I overheard Lauren-who-might-be-Finn's-mom and her stupid phone conversation, that I should do something about it, tell someone, that mothers aren't supposed to have romantic affairs with younger guys ...

And it all must show on my face because she smiles at me.

"Goodness, it's not that bad," she reassures me. "It's just my granddaughter, Sydney."

Sydney. A girl named Sydney. I don't know anyone named Sydney. Well, yes, Sidney Crosby, but I don't know him ... Clearly, or unclearly, my brain is still recovering from that moment of panic.

"I don't ..."

"She's going to be starting at the high school on Monday," says Mrs. Bart. She's smiling, but it's a smile that says there's a story here. "She's living with me for a while."

"Oh, I see. Well, that's nice for you."

Quick questions popping into my head: *Why is a teenage granddaughter living with you? Why is this delicate? What exactly do you want me to do? Why do you have this look on your face, like this is not good news? Why do I sense trouble ...?*

Bliss, I remind myself, *don't look too far ahead.*

"It is nice for me." Mrs. Bart finally smiles a real smile. "Sydney is one of my favourite people in this world. So smart, so talented. Her dad is my son Brandon, up in Ottawa. She's a competitive curler, you know. Competes at events all over the country. She wants to go to the Olympics one day."

This sounds promising. Curling, okay. My father grew up in a curling family, small town Ontario, bonspiels on the weekends, with prizes like turkeys and gift certificates to the local hardware store. "It's all physics," he told me once as we watched some big competition on TV. It was, too. Also, lots of yelling. "Not for wusses," he told me. "It's a lot harder than it looks." As I learned in our Grade 9 gym unit on curling that took place at the local club for two freezing hours. So, if Mrs. Bart's granddaughter Sydney is that good at it, I salute her.

"That's great," I say.

"Yes, it is. But she's taking this season off and living with me for a while." She looks at me now, and I can tell (ignoring The First Rule of Knitting) there's more to this story. "Bliss, she's pregnant. Due in November."

"Oh." I did not see that coming. "Oh, that's ..." Not quite sure how to respond. Skating a little here. But Mrs. Bart is ready to spill, so it turns out I don't have to say anything.

"She's a wonderful girl, Bliss. In fact, she reminds me a bit of you, with your talent." Did I mention Mrs. Bart is a retired elementary school teacher, used to encouraging and leading the young? "But things at home are a bit tough for Sydney right now, as you can imagine. Her mom is not dealing with it very well ..." Ah. The disappointed mom-who-is-also-a-daughter-in-law problem. "So, I suggested maybe she'd like to come and stay here, with me, and she could do her Grade 11 classes online, but, well, that's not Sydney."

I nod as if I'm following where this is going, which I'm not. "Oh, okay."

"'I'm not hiding at home,' she said. She's very social." Obviously. Pregnant, right? "So, I suggested she enrol at the high school for this semester, see how it goes."

I nod again, polite yet confused, and getting a bit worried, too. Where do I fit into this plan, exactly? "That sounds ... good."

"Yes, yes, it's a good plan, and I love having her around, and we've already connected with the midwives and all that," says Mrs. Bart. She might be trying to convince herself, or me, I'm not sure. "But I wondered, Bliss, if you could just have an eye out for her when she arrives at school. Just, maybe, make sure she's, you know, not alone there."

Ah. Mothers. Or in this case, a grandmother.

On my first day of junior kindergarten, Dad had to take me because Mom said she would cry too much and embarrass me. They told me this story years later and we all laughed about it, but I hugged her tight before going to bed that night, because I could just imagine her, watching Dad and me toddle off down the sidewalk toward my first day of school while she cried her eyes out at the window.

Mrs. Bart is telling me that she's a mother—okay, a grand-mother—and she's going to be standing at the window on Sydney's first day of school. This is something I understand.

"Oh, don't worry at all, Mrs. Bart. I'll watch for her, give her the scoop on where everything is. Anything she needs, I can help."

She reaches out and pats my hand. "I knew I could count on you, Bliss. Thank you so much."

"Happy to help." Yes, the Help Desk scores again.

Of course, this Sydney girl might not want my help, but I don't mention that to her grandmother, who is clearly relieved and counting on me.

So, on Monday morning, I throw a smile toward Sydney Bart, as she and her noticeable bump come through the classroom door with Ms. George and are directed to an empty desk. And she smiles back, just a little, then squares her shoulders (athlete, right?), sits down, and ignores the ripple of glances flowing around the room, including Bethany, who catches my eye and mouths: "Is she PREGNANT?"

6. PFFT PFFT PFFT

Anderson is killing it.

At lunch today, I told him I would come and watch if he wanted a cheerleading section.

"Don't come," he says. "Nobody comes to watch tryouts."

"Really?" I squint at him. This is new territory for us. I don't try out for teams, either. Caring Community Club is about my limit. "I would."

"Well, you're different." He smiles at me through his mouthful of chicken wrap, though.

So, fine, I don't actually walk into the gym and climb into the bleachers. Instead, after Tuesday classes are over and a suitable time has passed, I walk (which means I open the gym door a crack, slide through, remembering to slip off my backpack first so I don't make a clunk on the door) into the gym, and watch from the corner, hidden from view by the bleachers.

The guys are milling around now, and even from my distant corner, I can see the looks directed at Anderson, a newbie when it comes to athletic endeavour at our school. Also looking remarkably large in his size Triple-X Large shorts and Hillside Music Festival tee.

I feel my hands clenching. *Be nice to my friend, you jerks ...*

"Warm up those hands, guys." Mr. Coslov appears from the gym office, carrying a clipboard and pointing at the rack of volleyballs. "Grab a ball, find some space, keep the ball in the air. Go."

Anderson joins the throng. He waits his turn, picks up a ball, and ambles over to a spot on the floor, alone. Other guys are doing the same, but most are hanging in pairs, trios. Not Anderson, though. I see him give our friend James a nod as he passes him, but Anderson has clearly decided to go solo today.

Not sure why, but I feel this little spasm of something in my stomach, and realize that, yes, at this moment, I'm the Mom At The Window.

The guys get to work. *Pop, slap.* Balls into the air. Smack as one or two hit the floor.

I watch Anderson as he waits. Holds the ball, turns it over and around in his big hands a few times, as if he's getting to know it. And finally, when he's ready, he takes it gently on his fingertips, looks up, and launches it—*pfft, pfft, pfft*. Up, up, up. Soft, straight, high. The ball on his fingers—there's barely a sound as it floats up into the air, down for a brief touch of his fingertips, up into the air again.

It's a beautiful sight. I peer out around the bleachers at Mr. Coslov and I'm reassured to see that he's also watching Anderson in action, watching him intently, for longer than just a few seconds.

I let my breath out in a long sigh and slip back through the gym doors. Pretty sure Anderson just landed himself a spot on the Central High School Senior Boys volleyball team.

7. GYM CLASS

Sydney Bart isn't particularly sociable, and I don't want to look like I'm creeping her, so I just keep my distance with a half-smiling, I-am-friendly expression on my face whenever she happens to look my way.

So far, she's just smiled back, kind of a "I see you smiling at me" smile, and then she walks away.

Like at the end of homeroom that first day, for instance. She just stands up and walks out as soon as we're dismissed and heads off toward the Science wing, and since I'm on my way to English, I'm going in the other direction. But I see her in the hallway throughout the day, at her locker, minding her own business and not talking to anyone. She doesn't look lost or unhappy, either. Just in her own zone and perfectly okay.

I understand zones. I have my own zones, sometimes involving a quiet corner at String Theory and 50 grams of hand-dyed merino and a pair of super-smooth interchangeable needles. Sometimes, a few moments with a Mensa Sudoku puzzle. Even with Mrs. Bart's voice echoing in my head—*I knew I could count on you, Bliss*—I understand that Sydney doesn't need me marching up to her with her grandmother's instructions written clearly on my face. She walks through the hallways, back straight, eyes forward, blending in. Which is tough because, you know, there's that bump.

But then, on Wednesday morning, the time is suddenly just right: Phys Ed. Rainy day, so we're stuck inside, and the teachers open up the divider in the gym and announce we're going with Girls vs Boys badminton.

While Mr. Coslov and Mrs. Rice are giving us a few pointers, I slip over beside Bethany, who would in every other situation be my partner.

"Hey," I whisper, and she leans over, eyes still on the teachers. "I'm going to go with Sydney. Okay?"

Bethany looks over at Sydney, who is standing a bit apart on the side of the student huddle, big T-shirt hanging off her and not quite disguising the bump. Bethany knows all about my conversation with Mrs. Bart. "Go do good," she nods.

The teachers finally stop talking and I go to work, scooting past the quickly pairing-up crowd toward Sydney, who's still standing on the fringe. She sees me coming and raises her eyebrows.

"Partners?" she asks.

"Let's do it," I nod. "And I hope you know how to play badminton because I kind of suck at it."

It turns out Sydney does know how to play badminton. She *really* knows how. That birdie is torpedoed over the net and slams into the gym floor, over and over, as our opponents dive, twist, and flail. Not only that, but she can dive and twist with the best of them, no flail in sight. She's flicking and smashing us into win after win.

"Nice anticipation, Sydney," calls out Mrs. Rice.

"Crap!" mutters Devin. And Kalil. And Taz, he of the perfect proportions. And numerous other fairly athletic classmates, who can't believe they're getting the shit birdied out of them by the new girl. The new girl with the bump.

It's absolutely awesome.

And then we come up against a couple of the jock boys from the Gang of Five.

So here we are, Sydney and me, facing Cameron and Peter, and they're swaggering around the court, snapping the birdie back and forth like pros before we get started because, of course, they think they're going to demolish us. I'm not sure, but it's possible everybody is kind of watching us out of the corners of their eyes, interested in seeing this face-off.

"You sure you're up for this, ladies?"

Eew. Peter Abella just called us ladies.

"We wouldn't want to hurt you or anything." Cameron nods meaningfully at Sydney, which, for some reason, flips a switch in my brain.

"Dude, she's pregnant. She's not dying of some incurable disease."

The boys stare at me. Did I just say that out loud?

I turn my head slowly and look at Sydney, not sure what to say after that. I wish I could take it back.

But she's grinning at me as if I just said the funniest thing.

"You're not, are you?" I whisper. "I mean, dying of an incurable disease?"

"No, you're absolutely correct," she says. "Just pregnant. Six months pregnant. Look out, guys."

We kill them.

8. LUNCH GANG

"I knew you'd make it," I tell him. "I was there, you know."

"I know." Anderson takes a giant bite of his pita concoction, dripping mayonnaise and tomatoes all over his chin.

No way he knew.

"You knew? How?"

"Your little beady eyes peering around the corner of the bleachers." Chew, chew. Grinning at me.

"You think you're subtle," says Bethany. "You're not, you know. You always ..."

And she stops talking and looks at something over my head. Anderson keeps chewing, but he's looking at something over my head, too.

"Hi," says a voice behind me.

I swivel around. The voice is coming from Sydney Bart, my badminton hero.

"Hey, hi," I say.

Anderson and Bethany join in. It's hi all round as she looms over us, in her loose tunic sweater thing that kind of hides the bump that all four of us know is there.

"Want to join us?" I pull out the chair beside me, across from Anderson, so she can turn our triangle into a symmetrical square.

"Thanks."

"We were just congratulating Anderson for making the volleyball team," says Bethany, who has social skills far beyond mine, and knows how to get a conversation started. (If I were in charge of starting the conversation, I probably would have gone with something like, "How do you like it here so far?"—which would have forced Sydney to talk about herself. Awkward. Not for the first time, I'm grateful to Bethany for rescuing me from sounding like somebody's old auntie.)

"Cool," Sydney nods, reaching into her pack and pulling out a container of something that looks like quinoa. Rice. Some kind of grain with nuts and berries. She is obviously eating healthy, which makes Anderson's mayonnaise-adorned chin stand out even more. "Does the school have a good team?"

"It does now," says Bethany. "Anderson is like a pro when it comes to volleyball."

I expect Sydney to react to that—I mean, anyone looking at Anderson for the first time might think his bulk makes him the last thing from being good at any sport, other than maybe sumo wrestling—but she doesn't.

"I'm guessing you're a setter?" she says.

Anderson nods.

"Fingers like velvet," I say. "Mr. Coslov couldn't take his eyes off him."

"Ahhh, go on," he says through another mouthful of disgusting pita sandwich. Good athlete. Terrible table manners.

"Do you play?"

Sydney swallows another mouthful of her super-healthy lunch, nodding.

"Yeah, I was on my school team all through middle school, but then it started to conflict with curling season, so I let it go."

"Right, I heard you were a curler," I say, and then wonder if it's cool that I heard this from her grandmother. She doesn't seem to mind, though. In fact, she smiles. The second real smile I've seen from her today. (The first was during our high-five after demolishing Cameron and Peter this morning in gym.)

"Oh, great. My grandmother told you, didn't she?"

"Yes. Confession. She actually came into the store, and we were talking and she said you were moving in with her for a while, and that you were a famous curler." I shrug, trying to make it sound more like we were just talking, because I don't know this girl well enough to know how she'd react to hearing that her grandmother actually signed me up for a Look After My Pregnant Granddaughter assignment.

"Ha. Famous, no. But yes, I curl. A lot."

"Such a weird sport," says Bethany, who, I remember, was terrible at it during our gym excursion.

"Curling's not weird," Anderson says. "It's freaking hard."

"I agree. We did it in gym," I explain to Sydney. "The only people who could stay upright throwing the rock were the hardcore jocks and the kids who do competitive dance."

"Yeah, and that's not me," Bethany admits. It's true. Awesome in so many ways—creating papier-mâché volcanoes, drawing maps, scrapbooking—but physical stuff, no. Dancing, definitely not. She can't even ride a bike very well. "So, me and curling..." Dramatic pause, big eyes. "Not good."

Sydney actually laughs, but it's an "oh, you're cute" laugh.

"Anderson, you were pretty good at it," I remind him.

He shrugs. "Because I'm a great dancer, right?" He is, actually. At our Grade 8 grad dance, he wowed everyone. Girls, and a few boys, all wanted to be in our pack whenever the latest dance mix came on.

"I could curl this season if I wanted to."

Sydney says this as she focuses on digging out another forkful of quinoa and berries. The three of us glance at each other and try to think of something to say, but we don't need to because she pauses, shrugs, looks around at us.

"But I don't want to. I want to get this thing out of me and get my body and my life back," she says, mouth full. "So, you can stop dodging around it, okay, guys? I'm pregnant. Due in November. Living with my Gran because my mother is being stupid about it. It's all good."

Okay.

"Got it," I say.

"Good," says Bethany.

"Brave. And good for you." That's Anderson, someone who knows about being brave.

"Great, now that's out of the way, right?" Sydney nods, as if we've come to the end of a meeting and goes for the subject change. "So, what do people do for fun at this school?"

"Oh, well, let me tell you about the super fun after-school programs we have here at Central," Bethany, the organizer, the joiner, starts to roll. Anderson jumps in, of course.

I just listen. Eat my apple and listen.

Get my body and my life back. That's what Sydney said. *My mother is being stupid about it.*

It's all good.

I'm not so sure.

9. THE DARK HALLWAY, AGAIN

"Hi, Oscar!"

My mom can sound as if she has never been happier to see you walk through the door, and that's how she is right now, Wednesday night, as the first of the Knit & Natter group arrives.

You'd never know from her smiling face and welcoming voice that she's just spent the last hour behind the counter, on phone and computer, swearing under her breath, trying to deal with a complete mess-up of a long-awaited order from Sue, an unreliable and somewhat unfocused supplier ("Too many drugs," says Dad. I just think Sue spends too much time gazing into her favourite sheep's scary black eyes. We visited her farm once and all I remember is Sue, grey pigtails and a granny-squared poncho, nose to nose with a staring sheep named Bunny, cooing. The best skeins of grabby, sticky sheep yarn, of course, but just so weird. And doesn't seem to know how to deliver what she says she will, which drives Mom nuts.)

But Oscar, shy, skinny, in his usual uniform of jeans and handmade Icelandic Fair Isle pullover (Lett Lopi yarn in muted shades of grey), doesn't know any of this.

"Hi, Rowan!" he says, as if my mom is the best thing he's seen all day. I don't know much about Oscar (I know he works at the university, and, like I said, he's shy) but maybe my mom really IS the best thing he's seen all day.

I'm at the Help Desk, crocheting tonight. A display piece to showcase a new product, a corner-to-corner baby blanket with shiny, variegated yarn that slips through my fingers. It's a mindless, dreamy project, which means it's going quickly, and I'm feeling a bit mindless and dreamy, not really hearing Mom's muttered swearing at the counter. Oscar's arrival actually makes me jump.

"Hi, Bliss."

"Oh, hey, Oscar. Nice to see you."

Mom gives up on the Sue problem and comes out from behind the counter, carrying her knitting bag.

"Grab a chair, Oscar. I'm just going to go fill the kettle. Got your mug?"

"Sure do." From his backpack, he pulls out a thermal mug with the university logo. "Ready."

I'm securing my hook and wrapping up my work-in-progress so I can make room at the Help Desk table for K&Ners.

The door opens and two women sweep in, bringing a cloud of cool air and the sounds of passing traffic with them. Vela and Caroline, from the public library a couple of blocks away.

"Oscar! Hi! Hi, Bliss. Is your mom filling the kettle?"

"Yup." I move over to the counter as they fling coats over chairs, throw bags full of needles and yarn onto the table. Oscar seems to sit a little taller, obviously thrilled to see them. I wonder if there's a little romance brewing here between him and Vela. They're about the same age, both a bit shy ...

"How's your day been?"

"Pretty good. Yours?"

"Did you hear about council passing the bike lane thing?"

They're off, the three of them, chatting. Well, mostly Caroline, with her bright scarf, tunic, and leggings, hair caught up in a clip that leaves her grey fronds springing around her round face, and her voice that is all laughter. No need to lead a conversation when Caroline is in the room.

The door again, and Barbara (works at a manufacturing company, payroll or something) comes in. "Hi, everyone! Tracy not here yet?"

"Pretty sure I saw her parking in the lot next door as we came by," says Caroline.

Conversation gets louder, swirls around. This is the natter part. The knitting comes later.

Tracy (a young mother who likes to say this is her "oasis of Me in the middle of kiddie madness") arrives. Mother-and-daughter team of Annika and Enja arrives. Coats slung over the backs of their chairs. Knitting bags of every description—backpacks, like Oscar's, or cloth shopping bags, or specially designed carryalls, with spaces for needles, scissors, measuring tape. Yes, the knitting world is full of specialized equipment for its citizens. And this group considers itself citizens, for sure.

I hover at the end of the counter and listen to them, a smile of welcome pasted on my face, as instructed years ago by my commercially savvy parents. ("Always smile at the customers, Bliss. Makes them want to come back.") It's not hard. They're all so nice. I can just imagine them as teenagers, sitting around the school cafeteria ...

Mom comes back down the hall with her super-sized kettle, gives me a wink as she slips by.

"Hi, everyone!"

A chorus of greetings and the conversation gets even louder.

"Who else is coming?"

"What about Lauren, remember her?"

My ears perk up.

"I saw her parking down the street," says Annika.

Lauren. Possible mother of Finn. Voice from the dark hallway. I'm curious to see her, but also not sure I want to. If I see her face and there's a clear resemblance to the boy I know, then it will be real, and I'll have to get my head around the awkward fact that the mother of a boy I know is behaving badly ... and I know about it.

I glance at the window and see a woman outside, turned slightly away from us, and just a bit out of everyone's line of sight. I can see her clearly, though. A tall woman in a stylish three-quarter-length red coat with a bright plaid scarf wrapped around her neck. Shoulder-length, wavy brown hair. Black skinny jeans and boots with heels. Carrying a bag that might contain knitting.

With a phone pressed to her ear.

I watch her for a moment and see her grinning, saying something, listening, saying something else with a sort of smirk. She ends the call and is still smiling a little as she turns toward the entrance of String Theory, drops the phone into her pocket, and gets ready to push the door open.

But before she does, I slip away, down the hallway, past the bathroom and the storage room, toward my dimly lit window seat behind the curtain, around the corner, where no one can see me.

"Hi, Lauren. You made it! Great!" Mom.

49

"Yup, hi, everyone. Rowan, not sure I can stay very long tonight. Have to pick up my daughter from dance class. But I'm here for a while, anyway. Hope I haven't missed anything?"

"Not at all. We're just getting started," says Mom. "Kettle's about to boil, and we'll all get settled. Now, what's everyone working on?"

The voices are dulled a little by the curtain. I settle onto the window seat in my corner, with just the light of the kitchenette across from me, and pull out the baby blanket.

Like knitting, crocheting is soothing, regular, almost mechanical. Hook in loop, yarn around, pull through, over and over in a simple pattern of repetition. And this yarn is so smooth and soft, it's mesmerizing. I turn off the voices (which is hard, with Caroline bursting into laughter every thirty seconds or so) and let myself go mindless and dreamy again.

Mindless and dreamy. But every now and then, Finn Nordin, who is also tall and has wavy brown hair, drifts into my mind and drifts out again. I wonder—does he have a sister who dances?

10. CRAFTING FOR COMMUNITY CARE CLUB

"So, how do I sign up?"

I've been zoned out, head down, deep into a fascinating *New York Times* article I found on my phone about knitting, coding, and physics—yes, all three in the same article—so I don't notice Sydney until she's right in front of me, at my table set up in the gym for the September Clubs Bazaar (also known among Central students as "Clubs Bizarre," but I'm not sure the teachers know that). It's been pretty slow at our Crafting for Community Care (aka 3C Club) table. So slow that Charis—whose Cape Breton grandmother probably taught her how to hook rugs at birth—has taken a break and is strolling around, looking at the other clubs' displays.

"Hey, hi." I put down my phone and smile up at Sydney. "Really? You're interested in signing up?"

"Not sure yet." She picks up the flyer, designed by me—well, me and Dad, who can't keep his hands off any kind of marketing material—to reflect the opportunities available for anyone who (a) knits, crochets, quilts, hooks, or otherwise crafts, and who (b) wants to donate their time and creations to supporting those who will benefit.

"Hospital birthing unit," reads Sydney from the list of organizations who welcome our donations of baby blankets, and winter hats and scarves and mitts, and crafted toys. She raises an eyebrow and glances at me. Looks down at the list again. "Hospital neo-natal unit. Women in Crisis Centre." She glances back at me with a twisted smile. "Wow. Have I ever come to the right place."

Yikes.

I lean forward and point to a few other names on the list.

"And the Welcome Centre shelter, and the Humane Society, and the food bank ..."

"Oh, good. It's not all about me, then."

I don't know her that well, so it takes me a nanosecond to realize that she's joking. Thank goodness.

"It's all about, you know, giving back to the community." I shrug.

"Sure. Sounds good to me. And anyway, I have to do something or my grandmother will get on my case," she says, moving down the table to the sign-up sheet and grabbing the pen. "As you can probably imagine."

Yes, I'm pretty sure Mrs. Bart would speak up about getting

involved and doing good works. Maybe she already has, which is why Sydney found her way to my table.

Sydney and I are still in that moment—grinning down the table at each other about her grandmother—when I realize that two other people have stopped in front of me to read the flyer.

"So, what's the deal here?" asks one of them. "We knit stuff and donate it?"

Karlee and Adele. Finn Nordin's girlfriend and her sidekick. I don't know them really well because they came to Central from one of the other feeder schools up the hill, where the big houses are. Nice enough, I guess. Karlee is, well, quiet and smiley most of the time. Adele, on the other hand, always seems to be mad about something.

It was Adele who spoke, and it takes a moment to decipher her words because, first, I'm still giggling with Sydney about the powers of her grandmother to decree the doing of Good Works, and second, I've just realized that Finn is standing a little behind them, leaning in to pick up a flyer and starting to read. I can't help myself: I stare at him, looking for a resemblance to Knit & Natter Lauren.

Staring at people, especially a boy you don't know very well, is generally not recommended practice, I remind myself.

My eyes flick back to Adele and Karlee, who are both watching me and waiting for a reply. And looking as if they know that, as I was looking at their boy there, I was wondering if he's the Finn with the Bad Mom and the dancing little sister.

Yes, thoughts spin through my head at lightning speed. Computer calculation speed. It's exhausting sometimes, really, it is.

"Exactly. You can do stuff on your own, and we organize donating it." I go into Club Leader mode and focus just on the two girls in front of me, ignoring Finn, who is still standing a little behind Karlee. "Or you can come to the club on Thursdays at lunch hour in Mrs. Badali's room. You get participation points if you come to the meetings."

I say all this with my official Club Leader smile and voice of explanation, all while looking up at them, and I can already tell they're not impressed. Well, no, that's not quite true. They are impressed with how geeky I sound. But since I'm used to this, it doesn't bother me. Neither one says anything as they glance from the flyer to me and back at the flyer, twin expressions of "what?" on their faces.

"If you come to the club, we can help with choosing projects and patterns. And if you're a beginner, we can show you how to get started, and the different patterns and stitches and stuff. Or you can just work on your own."

I end my speech and look at them, each in turn. Karlee smiles faintly and looks confused. Adele just looks as if she doesn't even want to be here.

54

"Thursdays at lunch?"

A new voice.

I look up at Finn Nordin, who now steps up beside Karlee and speaks to me directly. His eyes are blue, so blue, and he has perfect teeth. Wavy brown hair, well-trimmed. There's a little white scar on one cheekbone, close to his eye. I have no idea why I'm paying attention to all these details.

"Yes, Thursdays at lunch in Mrs. Badali's room."

"We could do that, Karlee," he nudges her.

"You'd go to a knitting club?" Karlee snorts, clearly a non-believer in the joys of dipping into a yarn stash and making something useful.

He shrugs. "Hey, it's for a good cause, right?"

The girls now snort-laugh together, but he just grins at them, flaps the flyer, and turns to me.

"Sounds like a great cause. We'll see, okay? Do we have to sign up today?"

Finn Nordin is talking to me, and all I can see is the woman in the red sweater, smirking into her phone.

"No, uh, no, you don't have to." I gather myself, focus on the next stitch, basically. "You can join any time, and you can also just work on a project on your own and donate it through the club. Whatever you want."

"Oh, come *on*, Finn," laughs Karlee as she turns to me. "No offence, Bliss. I know knitting is cool and it's for a good cause and everything, right? But this guy isn't a knitter."

"Hey, I like to try new things," he defends himself. "Also, in case you didn't know, my mother is all into this knitting club thing she just joined. And she wants Ava to sign up for the kids' club, too. At the store downtown."

Like the tiny pieces of an Enigma Machine falling into place, the code is slowly being revealed. I can't take my eyes off him because somewhere behind him, I see Lauren, the woman I think is his mother, hear her in the hallway, hear her last night, talking about picking up her daughter from dance. Ava. Is Ava his little sister? Does Ava dance?

"That's your parents' store, isn't it?" Adele asks, and three pairs of eyes are suddenly focused on me.

"Yes, it is. String Theory."

Finn laughs out loud. "Really? That's the name of the store? That is the best name ever."

"Whatever." Adele clearly has no sense of humour. "Look, we need something with participation points. Are we going to look around some more, guys, or what?"

"Sure. Thanks," Finn nods at me. "We'll let you know."

"Thanks, Bliss," says Karlee. Okay, I appreciate the good manners, but she's already moving on, her hand on Finn's arm, dragging him off. Adele just ignores us all and walks away.

Their pod of three slows briefly at the next table (Chess Club), where they take a quick look and then just keep walking.

"I like that guy," says someone. I had totally forgotten about Sydney, who was at the end of the table with the sign-up sheet, watching us the whole time. "A guy who knits. That's cool. Not sure about those girls, though."

"Oh, they're okay."

"You're way too nice," says Sydney. "I signed your list. See you on Thursday." She grins. "My gran is going to be so happy about this."

And she's off. I watch her walk through the gym with the easy, rolling stride of an athlete. She passes groups of people standing around tables, or just talking, and she doesn't see their glances. Or maybe she does, and she just doesn't care. The Pilates Club catches her attention and she moves in for more information. I bet she's great at Pilates ...

The chair beside me scrapes across the floor and Charis plops down.

"Anything happen while I was gone?" she asks.

"Nope," I shrug. "Not really."

That is not true, of course. But I'm not going to explain it to her.

11. AUNTIE BRYN

"So? How have the first few weeks gone? How's that dishy friend of yours doing?"

Auntie Bryn is stretched out on our couch with a glass of white wine resting on her stomach. Her nails are bright red this week, and the effect of crystal, shimmering wine, and in-your-face nails is perfect (and she knows it).

Dishy friend. Dishy friend ...

"You know!" She sees my confusion and clarifies. "Anderson. I just want to hug him every time I see him."

Oh! Anderson. Of course. For a minute, I had this weird feeling she was looking inside my head at the image of Finn Nordin, blue eyes and perfect teeth, standing at my table in the gym, laughing with me about the name of the store. This image has been floating around in my head a lot over the past few days.

"He's great, actually." I put down my hook and yarn to take

a sip of my tea. (Mom: "No, Bryn. Bliss is not allowed to have a glass of wine with you.") "He tried out for the volleyball team for the first time and he made it. Very exciting."

"Brilliant." Auntie Bryn takes a sip. "And what about you? Trying out for any teams?"

Snort laugh. "Uh, no." I pick up my hook and return to experimenting with the chart for a corner-to-corner crocheted blanket with a giant Toronto Maple Leafs logo. It's harder than you might think. All those points ...

Auntie Bryn watches for a moment, silent, until I glance up at her.

"Nothing wrong with a little athletic endeavour," she says. Of course, Auntie Bryn runs marathons and, like most runners, she thinks everyone should be in the cult with her.

"Oh, let her be." Mom plops down beside me on the loveseat and leans in to see my progress, her own wine glass in hand. "Looks good, honey. Honestly, Bryn, just because you're running up and down Yonge Street with thousands of marathon freaks every year and showing off your great legs."

"Yes, they are."

"Yes, they are. And you're a fine runner and I was a great tennis player and Patrick skates like Connor McDavid, but Bliss is her own girl and will pursue sports or not. And high school is not the only place to do that, so just back off."

Auntie Bryn makes a face at her, but then they're laughing together and talking about their high school memories of that kid who was such a star basketball player and is now running a chain of grocery stores. The stories start flowing. Two sisters, a grade apart. Sisters and friends.

And Auntie Bryn is my friend, too. She and I make an annual pilgrimage to the Canadian National Exhibition, just her and me ("We are CNE compatible," she says.). We took the train to Ottawa when I was ten, to stay in a hotel and visit the Science and Technology Museum, the Aviation and Space Museum, art galleries. I remember standing with her in the National Gallery, surrounded by forty audio speakers, each one broadcasting a different voice singing a part in a Tallis motet. Auntie Bryn brings the magic.

"If I had a daughter," she said to me once, "I would want her to be you, Bliss."

Auntie Bryn doesn't have kids. She doesn't have a husband, either, anymore. Stefan, her husband, died a year before I was born.

"When I look at you, Bliss, I think of Stefan," she told me once, years ago, when we were up in my room, looking through the family album, and suddenly there was a photo of them in a canoe. Young and laughing and strong. "He faded out of this world, and you burst into it."

Auntie Bryn says things like this, heavy things. Real things. Hard things. I love her for it.

She also made sure I didn't have to go through life with the name Guinevere, so I am her servant, forever.

"But seriously, Bliss," she says, now that the high school memories conversation has wrapped up, and she and Mom are leaning back, sipping wine and enjoying some Sunday evening downtime as Dad gets supper ready. "Your love life. I mean, really, what's happening?"

I make another correction on my Toronto Maple Leafs logo stitch chart.

"Oh, nothing to report there," I say, and take a big slurp of tea.

12. MATH CONTEST

"Okay, guys," says Mr. Wenzik in math class on Monday morning. "I have news."

This is almost as good as Mr. Wenzik saying something like, *Okay, guys, I have a quick quiz here, just to see where you are with those quadradic equations.*

And then his eyes swivel to me, and to someone at the back, and then back to me.

He smiles.

Hmmm.

"I'm happy to announce that two students from this class will be representing Central at the Annual University of Waterloo Grade 11 Math Contest and Math Olympics."

There's a small rustle of interest, but not really, because first of all, everyone knows that Math Contest and Math Olympics fall into the category of Math Nerds Only. And second, my classmates already know that I'm the poster girl for Math Nerd, so ...

"Congratulations, Bliss," says Mr. Wenzik with a nod and a smile.

"Of course," Bethany says, ventriloquist-style, without moving her lips.

And then Mr. Wenzik smiles to the back of the room. "And Finn. Congratulations to you, too."

Moment of silence. Shocked silence? No, not really. We all know Finn is really good at math. It's just that he's quiet about it. You know, he doesn't answer questions out loud like I do (which, in my defence, is something I do without really knowing I'm doing it. Sorry, but that's the truth.).

So there's a moment, and then—while Mr. Wenzik goes into the speech about how prestigious this contest is, what a great opportunity it is, blah, blah, blah—there's a rustle of movement as people turn to look at Finn and me to see our reaction.

Well, my reaction is pretty well what you might expect. I'm not surprised. We all wrote the qualifying test the first week of September and I haven't given it a thought since then, because it was challenging, okay, yes, it was challenging, but I still knew I'd done well on it.

But Finn—I glance back at him, and he's looking at me. He shrugs, smiles, tips his head a little to the side, as if to say, "Sorry, you're stuck with me." So I shrug as if to say, "Same."

Adele, sitting beside Finn, is looking at me, too. And she's not smiling. For some reason, she doesn't like me. Maybe she's like a guard dog for Karlee?

In any case, as Mr. Wenzik continues with his little public relations speech about the contest, and as Bethany raises an eyebrow at me ("Finn Nordin?"), and as the rest of the class listens with growing boredom and restlessness, I turn back to the front and consider the fact that Finn Nordin and I might be spending some time together in the near future, and this could get complicated.

"So, would you be able to drop in here at the end of the day, please, you two? I'd like to go over some preparation we need to do, okay? Bliss? Finn?" Mr. Wenzik wraps up and gives us both that teacher look, before turning to the whiteboard and grabbing a marker. "Fine. Let's get on with today's material. Page 58 in your textbook, please. Question one."

Yes, we're going to be working together, and I do feel weird about this because there's the whole scene-from-a-bad-romance mother, and the unsettling power of those blue eyes, not to mention the girlfriend and the girlfriend's cranky friend.

But then, as I bite my lip to keep from calling out the answer to the question Mr. Wenzik just wrote on the board, I take a deep breath and remind myself of the principle I live by.

I'm not going to look too far ahead.

13. BLEACHERS

"So? What's the deal? How much time are you going to be spending with Finn Nordin?"

Bethany is already in the bleachers, waiting for me after school. We're picking up Anderson and heading to String Theory to sort skeins of old, overlooked yarn into donation piles for the 3C Club, a little goodwill outreach that Mom and Dad suggested to the school. They also promised us pizza.

I'm still climbing up the clanking metal steps toward her when she starts pestering me.

"Sheesh, let me sit down at least." I drop my pack at my feet and sit beside her on the hard wooden seat. Why did she think the nearly top row was the best place to wait?

"Sorry. Need to know. This is *big*. So?"

Bethany has her own style. My dad calls it "a flair for the dramatic." I think of it more as her tendency to spend way too much time watching reality shows and transferring that out-there style into her life. And sometimes into my life, too.

"It's not big," I tell her, my eyes on a group of guys down on the gym floor, standing around outside the equipment room, waiting to get their uniform shirts. A group of guys that includes Anderson.

As always, he looks chill. Big, beefy, Triple-X Large, of course, but chill. He's standing beside James, a tall, muscular guy who will star on the basketball team during the Winter term. And the track team next Spring, once the snow melts and the track dries up. A natural athlete, and the same very nice boy we've known since kindergarten.

I am secretly crossing my fingers that there's a uniform shirt in Anderson's size because, otherwise, it could be awkward for him.

"So? So? Come on!"

I drag my eyes away from Anderson and give her a look. "What? It's just a contest thing. And a math activities thing. It's nothing."

"Nothing. Right."

It really isn't that big a deal. In fact, it's a bit silly, if you ask me. Writing the contest, okay, that's fine. I love that stuff. But then hanging around at the university for the afternoon to do team challenges and interact socially with other math nerds? Yeah, no.

Of course, one of the math nerds is Finn Nordin. And we'll be travelling together from school with Mr. Wenzik in the school van. And practising together beforehand—if you can call running through challenging math questions "practising," that is.

"So, what did you and Finn talk about with Wenzik?"

"Actually, it was just me and Wenzik."

Finn wasn't there. He had somewhere else to be, apparently, and by the time I got to the classroom, he was gone.

"So, you know the drill," Mr. Wenzik said. And I do know the drill, because I've been writing math contests under his direction since I was in Grade 9. There was a sort of Math Olympics thing that year, too, held at an independent school in Hamilton.

Oh, yes. I remember it well. I was part of a school contingent consisting of me, Rebecca Yeung, Barry Michi, and (thankfully) Anderson, who is not only surprisingly good at volleyball, but also surprisingly good at math, when he wants to be. They had us doing team competitions for prizes (one was a twelve-sided Rubik's Cube, I remember). Lunch was this massive buffet of pizza, make-your-own sandwiches, and vegetarian lasagna, and that was probably the highlight. Our team didn't win—Barry and Rebecca don't like each other, for some unexplained reason, and Anderson and I were distracted by their bickering. Until it became funny to us, and then we were just totally focused on the entertainment they provided. Mr. Wenzik was distracted by some old friend who teaches at one of the other schools and didn't really care, so, yeah, it was a disaster for Central High.

This will be different, he tells me. Serious, well organized by the Mathematics Department at the University of Waterloo. Representatives from schools around the region and maybe even beyond.

"No Rubik's Cubes?" I ask him.

"Probably not," he says, but then he grins at me. He remembers Grade 9, too. "But in the meantime, I'll send you both practice documents and the itinerary. I'll be driving us there in the school van, so you'll both need permission forms signed and all that. It's too bad Finn couldn't be here this afternoon to sort out these details, but maybe you two could find some time to work together? Do some prep? Go over the practice questions?"

"Sure."

I picture Finn and me, sitting in this classroom, doing math problems together, Karlee and Adele seated a few desks away, watching us like hawks.

"Great. You're the veteran here, Bliss, so you can take the lead. Finn's never wanted to get involved before, so this is good. New blood, and a strong team we've got, with you two. I'm looking forward to this." He grins at me again. Yes, Mr. Wenzik is also a math nerd, and I bet getting a day away from school to attend a special event, where most of the work is done by the students and the contest organizers, probably has a certain appeal.

So now, sitting beside Bethany in the bleachers, I don't feel like getting into the specifics of my conversation with Wenzik. Especially not the practising-with-Finn part.

"It's just one more thing to do," I tell her, eyes focused on Anderson. He and James are now laughing about something.

"I wonder what Karlee and Adele think about you hanging out with their boy," Bethany says, raising her eyebrows at me in expectation. Reality show, right?

"It's math, Bets. A school-related math thing. That's all."

I turn back to the scene unfolding on the gym floor: Anderson and James are at the front of the line now, and Mr. Coslov comes out of his office with two uniform shirts, blue and yellow, school colours, and a big number on the back. A conversation, then Anderson reaches for a shirt and holds it up for a look (it definitely looks Triple-X Large). Smiles, nods his head, waits as James gets his shirt (also large, but not as large as Anderson's), and the two step away and say something to each other and laugh again. James heads for the door and Anderson looks up at the bleachers because he knows we're there, waiting for him.

Let's go, he nods, and waves at us.

So, much has been accomplished here. Anderson now has at least one volleyball friend to go along with his new uniform, and Bethany now knows that it's all just math nerd business between me and Finn.

Good. All good.

69

14. 3C CLUB

"That's a lot of wool," says Mrs. Badali from her desk as Anderson and I come through the classroom door on Thursday morning before the bell, each carrying two large, clear garbage bags stuffed with skeins and balls of all colours. Fortunately, Dad gave us a drive, because I can't imagine the scene we'd cause—Anderson and me walking through the neighbourhood dragging our giant yarn-filled balloons.

Anderson, Bethany, and I spent a few hours on Monday night at the store, sorting old yarn (translation: finding a new home for unsold-after-two-years yarn because Mom says she wants to make room for new inventory) of all descriptions into piles based on weight and colour. It's a gorgeous fibre mishmash and I just want to dive into it, squish it in my hands, mix and match it, loop it onto needles, and knit my brains out.

But no. Steady there, Bliss. This is yarn intended for the

Crafting for Community Care Club and the mostly beginner crafters, who will join us in doing good works and getting school participation points, an essential ingredient of the Clubs Bizarre.

"So generous of your parents, Bliss." Mrs. Badali shakes her head, impressed with the amount. "Please thank them for us."

"I will." And yes, I will, but I know exactly what my parents will say. *Nonsense. Just doing our part* ... It wouldn't surprise me if some of the yarn here isn't as old or unwanted as Mom made it out to be.

So, at lunch break, Anderson and I make our way back to Mrs. Badali's classroom for the official start of the 3C Club. We find Charis already in action, meeting and greeting some of the people who signed up.

"Fantastic!" Charis says to us as she gazes at the bags, now on display at the front of the room. She's in heaven. Yarn stash heaven.

"We're going to knit all that?" A Grade 9 girl sitting at one of the desks is staring at the bulging, colour-stacked bags and looks as if she's about to stand and run.

"Probably not all of it. Don't worry," Anderson reassures her. "But there's lots to choose from and you can start small." Anderson recognizes panic when he sees it. The girl looks at him as if running might still be a good idea. Anderson sometimes has that effect on people.

"Right, let's get going," says Charis. She has the sign-up sheet and starts checking attendance. Yes, attendance, because people get participation points for this. We're very organized in our extra-curriculars here at Central. "Okay, who's here? Amanda Perrault?"

It's all very orderly. I'm leaning on a desk off to the side, mostly zoned out and trying not to think too much about who might show up, when Sydney appears.

"What did I miss?" She ignores the glances of the other students, who are listening to Charis, but also noting the latecomer and her bump.

"Just getting started," I tell her.

Attendance done, Charis introduces herself and points out Anderson and me (we're the "teachers" here). She goes into her spiel about the goal of the club, and asks everyone's level of expertise.

"Do you know how to knit?" I ask Sydney.

"Nope. But how hard can it be?"

Well, in fact, it can be very hard, if you're into multi-colour graphs and chevron lace stitch, or travelling vine stitch, for instance, but Sydney's right: what we're doing in 3C Club is not going to be hard.

It's a fun hour, actually. Matching everyone up with a yarn they like, handing out the easy patterns for scarves, baby blankets, hats. Distributing needles from our supply box and then leading everyone through the art of using a chair-back to wind a skein into a ball, casting on, reading the pattern we've chosen, managing the needles and yarn. There's a lot of ripping out and starting over. Also a lot of laughs, because Charis is one of those people who carries light around with her (and thank goodness for that, because I don't have this gift).

Anderson has bonded with Amanda, the nervous minor niner, and he actually makes her giggle. Sydney and I park at a desk and I walk her through the first steps, which she picks up easily. She has four rows of a simple K2–P2 scarf pattern completed in no time, with pretty good tension and only one dropped stitch.

"My grandmother will be so proud."

"She will be. It's true."

Mrs. Badali sits at her desk the whole time, eating her lunch and scrolling her computer (work or pleasure, not sure, don't care. Poor teachers who get stuck having to supervise extra-curriculars during their lunch hours can do whatever they want).

And then, just as everyone is carefully following Charis's instructions to wrap a few lengths of yarn around their started project, stick the needles into the ball, and carefully stow it in a bag so it doesn't unravel—and Amanda drops everything and nearly bursts into tears, until Anderson picks it up and says,

"See? No stitches lost. It's fine"; and just as Sydney tells me she'll have the scarf finished by Monday—just at that moment, Karlee and Adele and Finn show up at the door and Karlee says, "Oh, no! We're so sorry we're late! Can we still join?"

15. WALKING AND TALKING

Sydney's text comes in just as I'm settling down with the math contest prep documents that Wenzik emailed me. A few hours of playing with math questions before heading to the store for my Saturday Help Desk shift did sound like a perfect way to spend the morning—until the text came, and then I rethought my priorities.

I need a walk. Can you come?

Pretty sure I hear the pleading voice of Sydney's grandmother in the background.

Sure. Meet at The Boathouse?

See you in 15

So, a walk with the pregnant exile it is.

"I had to get out of the house," she says, as we rendezvous on a bench outside the local ice cream place, now closed for the season.

It's chilly, but not awful. We're both bundled up, but the sun is shining and if someone would bring a cup of tea from the closed tearoom, I'd be quite content. Sydney isn't content, though. She has a scarf wrapped around her neck, and an oversized jacket with a curling logo on the sleeve, and her arms are crossed as she slumps on the bench, her eyes on the water.

I wait, because although I do spend a lot of time focused on inanimate things like yarn and needles and math problems, I also know when someone has something on their mind. Years of being friends with Anderson has taught me that sometimes you just have to wait for the moment and be ready for it. Ready to jump in.

Grade 8, the picnic table in the park near his house. Anderson, with his head buried in his arms, has just told me his big secret—which wasn't really a secret to me—and he's so confused and unhappy.

"It's okay, Anderson. It's going to be okay. What do you want? What do you want to happen next?"

"I don't know. I just want to be happy. I want to tell Mom and have her understand. I just want to tell people and have them still like me. And nobody say, That's weird, or That's wrong." He lifts his head and looks at me, then down, deep down, away from me. Hiding, almost. "You get it, don't you, Bliss?" Almost a whisper.

"I get it." I lean over and put my face right up close to his, so he can't help looking at me. Put my arm as far as I can around his big, shaking shoulders. "I get it, Anderson. I always got it."

(And for the record, his mom totally understood.)

So, I wait for Sydney, and it takes a while.

It takes us until we've walked all the way past the bandshell, and the deserted playing fields. Past the place they store the canoes. Past the swings and the playground. Past a community garden, where people are at work, preparing their little patch for the winter. Past the dog park, where we stand watching three adorable doodles of various sizes play a wild game of tag, while their owners stand chatting, holding coffees and leashes. All the way to the end of the trail, where you either have to turn around, or venture out onto the sidewalk of a busy street, and weave a path back through neighbourhoods. We turn around.

It takes us working through conversation that includes knitting, curling, how much our school is different from her school in Ottawa. (She goes to an independent school there. Wears a uniform. Has to attend a secular worship service every morning before classes start. The homework load is brutal.) A podcast she listens to (movie reviews). A podcast I listen to (latest scientific fun facts).

It takes us until we've been silent for a few minutes of walking and we're almost back to our bench at The Boathouse. Just as

I'm about to break the silence and tell her I really have to get going because the Help Desk is calling, and my parents will be disappointed if I don't show (in fact, I'm pretty sure that buzzing of the phone in my pocket is my mom asking where I am).

It's right about then that Sydney says: "You know what I can't stop thinking about?" She waves her hand over her bump.

"That makes perfect sense." I say what she needs to hear. I also sincerely believe it. How could you walk around all day, carrying a growing human inside you and not think about it constantly? The thought fills me with horror. Not just the growing human, but the how-it-got-there part, too.

"No, not that. Not *this*." She flits her hand over her middle, as if trying to whisk it away. "I can't stop thinking about the fact that I haven't told him."

Him? The guy. The *father*.

"Um ..."

We've stopped walking and we're standing on the path in front of our bench. Looking out at the river, which is flowing well today. It looks cold. Everything feels cold, feels like the sun is outgunned.

"So, he doesn't know?"

She shakes her head. "I don't think so. I haven't told him. My parents said I shouldn't." She stares out at the water for a moment. "I haven't told him—yet. But he has to know. He'll see that I'm not competing with the team. My parents know who he is, but I never told anyone else. My coach and teammates know about this, but not ... not who." That hand wave over her bump again, dismissive. "He's going to see that I'm out for the season, and I just know someone's going to tell him, and he'll figure it out."

"Where is he?" I'm confused. "Surely he's noticed that you're not at school. And if any of your friends know ..."

"No, you've got it wrong," she turns to me then. "It's not a boy at school. It's a guy I know from curling camp last year. He's Norwegian. His name's Magnus Haugen."

"Oh." Wow. That's a name, all right.

"We've known each other for a few years." She plops down on the bench, staring off at the water, and the words are starting to flow. "We met at a curling camp in Halifax a few years ago. And then a spiel in Ottawa. And then at this camp in Switzerland last year. We were on the same team for the shoot-out. Did drills together and stuff like that. Off-ice stuff, too."

I'm not completely sure what she's referring to, all this curling stuff, so I just sit there beside her, nod my head, and let her ramble on because, clearly, that's why she needed this little meeting today.

"And then they paired us up for mixed doubles." She's in memory mode now, somewhere else. Back in Switzerland, I guess. Smiling. Totally unaware of the sun just starting to creep through the clouds and make sparklies on the flowing water of the Speed River ...

"There were social events, and we were watched like hawks, of course. But there was this one night, at the end. We slipped out and went for a walk, and we talked and talked. And he had the keys to the team van. We sat there, just talking and talking about everything. School, our families, curling. Life. Us." A long pause, and I know she's way, way, far away, in the past, over an ocean.

"We bonded," she says, finally, and hearing her own words seems to break the spell. Her voice changes. "Yeah. We bonded, all right."

She doesn't go into any details, much to my relief. Instead, she sits up a bit, coming back to our bench by the river on a cold Saturday afternoon.

"So, I'm here, and *this* is happening, and he's back home in Norway, and that's how it is." She turns to me. "I have no idea why I'm telling you all this. You're very easy to talk to, do you know that?"

I shrug. "Help Desk. That's me."

"Well, whatever. Thanks for listening. I know we don't know each other very well, but, well, thanks."

"You're welcome."

My phone buzzes again and this time I take it out. Yup, Mom.

"Sorry," I say, and I mean it. She's hunched over, staring at the water and far, far away. "I'm really sorry, but I have to go. I'm on duty at the store this afternoon. Help Desk."

Sydney laughs at that. "You need to wear a sign."

And then, as we stand up and start walking up the path toward the street, she says, "I feel better. Thanks, Bliss. Screw Magnus Haugen and his Viking good looks."

Which is an unfortunate choice of words, of course, so we both start to giggle.

16. MAKING PLANS

"That is way too much homework for a Monday," Bethany complains as we leave math class on Monday morning.

"You can never have too much math homework," I say.

We're swimming along in the two-way flow that signals the change between classes. For us, that means English, and our current unit on Shakespeare. *Macbeth*. I'm not enjoying this unit or this play, and it occurs to me that you can have too much English homework any day of the week. But, when it comes to math ...

"Geek-speak." Bethany doesn't like math.

"Hey, Bliss?"

A new voice. A male voice. Behind us. We both turn but we keep walking, because stopping in the middle of the class-change flow is not only frowned upon, but physically dangerous.

Finn Nordin has caught up with us and we are now a trio,

which means we're too wide for the stream. Bethany wisely surges ahead. I'm pretty sure she does this because she thinks she can hear better in front of us than behind us. I can tell by her puffed-up cheeks that she's grinning.

"Hi." I've never said his name and it doesn't seem called for. (And why am I even thinking about this?) We're now walking side-by-side down the hallway and no one seems to be paying attention to us. (And why am I even thinking about this?) Except for Bethany, of course. Okay, maybe a few people are flicking glances our way.

"Listen, I was wondering if you'd be able to meet up after school for half an hour or so, to go over the math contest thing. Make a plan for prepping," he says. "Maybe in the library?"

"Sure, good idea." I glance around quickly, just to see if Adele and Karlee are anywhere in sight. Nope. He's flying solo.

"Sorry I couldn't be there that first day," he says. "Wenzik sent me the stuff and I was looking at it over the weekend." I glance at him and he smiles. "Pretty heavy stuff, eh?"

"Yeah, I was looking at it, too." I don't tell him that it didn't seem that heavy to me, but that's because I've had years of practice, honing my math weirdness into something that looks normal. It's not normal, as every teacher I've ever met keeps telling me.

"I'll be following your lead," he says, as if he had been

reading my mind. "I know you're the wiz here. Looking forward to working with you. Should be fun, eh?" And he smiles again. He has a nice smile and seems to use it a lot. "See you after school."

"Yup, see you then," I nod, smile, try not to notice that by now, more than one pair of eyes have clocked us walking down the hallway together, and that Bethany is slowing her pace so much that I'm likely to step on her heels any moment.

He waves goodbye, cuts off into the stream going the other way and is gone.

Bethany is beside me even before I can process how quickly we've arrived at the door of our English class.

"That was nice," she says.

"Yes. Math stuff," I reply. "I know how much you like math stuff."

"Right. Math stuff." She's grinning, and I'm pretty sure she already has us married, the parents of two adorable kids, and living in a nice house with a two-car garage. She watches way too many romcoms. "He's nice, isn't he?"

"Yes, he is." Truth. He seems like a very nice boy. (I sound like my grandmother in my head.)

"Lucky you."

"It's just the math contest, Bets. That's all."

She grins but doesn't say anything, and I don't either, as we stow our packs, pull out our laptops and ratty copies of the play, and prepare for Ms. George to launch into whatever nitpicking topic of discussion she's going to subject us to today.

He *is* nice, I think. And nice kids usually have nice parents, don't they?

17. LIBRARY

He's already there when I arrive, at the best table by the window, tucked up in the corner near the magazine rack. Everyone likes it because you can actually talk and not disturb anyone working in the study carrells on the other side of the room.

"Hey," he says as I drop my pack and sit down. "This good?"

"Perfect. Sorry I'm late."

I was delayed by Anderson catching up to me in the hallway on his way to volleyball practice.

"First game next week. You'll be there?"

"I'll be there." Duh.

"And I hear you're off to talk math with the other math wiz," he grins at me.

Thank you, Bethany, the human equivalent of Reply All.

"Yes. Yes, I am." I glance at him. "So?"

"So, nothing. Just, you know, you hanging out in the library with a boy. New territory."

"Math, Anderson. It's math."

The only boy I hang out with is Anderson. Everyone knows this—my friends, my parents, even Auntie Bryn. I find boys interesting from afar—you know, intriguing examples of good physical proportions, like Taz Fenwick. Or annoying sources of entertainment, like Cameron Tellez and Peter Abella—but, full disclosure, never been kissed. Never wanted to be. I like to hide behind needles and yarn. And math problems. And Anderson.

Yes, boys scare me a little. Maybe more than a little.

So, meeting up with an unknown quantity like Finn Nordin, even for the most ordinary reason, that we're both competing in a math contest ...

"Hey. He's one of the nice guys," Anderson says. "Go have fun doing math."

Anderson knows me so well.

"And," he continues, "he has a girlfriend, so you're golden. Tell me how it goes. Later!" And he's off down the hall that leads to the gym.

I climb the stairs to the library, mulling over that "girlfriend" and "golden" comment, and realize that now I'm late. Maybe he's gone?

Nope. He's there.

"No problem." Finn says when I apologize for keeping him waiting. He already has his laptop open, I'm guessing with the information and practice-question documents Wenzik sent us already up on his screen. "Wish they'd let us bring coffee in here."

"Or tea, but yeah. That would be civilized."

"This school needs a Starbucks."

I smile because this is something Anderson, Bethany, and I have talked about a million times. A little café. A Tim's. A Starbucks. The cafeteria just doesn't have the same appeal, and, of course, you can just forget bringing food or drink into the library.

"I agree completely."

"Math and hot beverages, right?" He shrugs with his hands in the air as if this is a truth everyone knows. "Next time, we'll have to meet up somewhere else. The café on Quebec Street is nice."

I know the one. It's right across from String Theory. In my mind, I see us sitting at one of the little tables with our math problems and our hot beverages.

"Maybe Saturday," he suggests. "Would you be free on Saturday? To meet up somewhere?"

"Um ..." I'm thinking. Saturday is Help Desk day.

"I have hockey practice a couple of times a week, so I can't stick around after school." He shrugs. "And sometimes I have to be home for my little sister, when my mother's late at work." All this information is building up in my head, along with the questions: *Is your little sister a dancer? Does your mother have a boyfriend?*

He notices the look on my face and immediately backtracks. "But, if this is the only time you can meet up ..."

"You could come to String Theory, our store, on Saturday afternoon." I blurt it out just as the idea pops into my head—out of nowhere.

"String Theory?" he grins. "The knitting store?"

"Yeah, I'm there every Saturday afternoon. Help Desk."

It could be okay, I guess. Me and Finn sitting at a table doing math problems, while the usual String Theory regulars come by for their Help Desk rescue. I can see it. Mom and Dad would love it.

"Sounds good," he grins. "Let's do it, then. Help Desk at String Theory. Maybe I'll learn something about knitting." Something flashes across his face. "Hey. I can check it out for Ava. She's my little sister. My mom wants her to sign up for some kids' program there."

"Actually, my mom and I run the kids' program, so I could give you the info then, too."

"Better and better. Sounds like we have a plan."

And that's exactly the moment Karlee and Adele show up to find us smiling at each other about our Saturday plans, ignoring our laptops, and clearly not doing anything related to math contest prep.

"Hi, guys. Done yet?" asks Karlee.

Adele's eyes flick to me and back to Finn. "Can we go?"

"We've hardly started," he protests, but he must be used to being pestered by his female posse, because he just grins at them.

"Clearly." Adele looks at me, back to Finn, back to me. So meaningful. She has such a way of sounding mad all the time.

"That's okay. We'll just wait for you." Karlee pulls out one of the other chairs and makes herself comfortable. "I've got geography homework."

Adele sighs loudly, sits down in the other chair, and pulls out some textbook. I pull up math contest practice pages on my laptop.

"So, do you want to just run through Part A and see how it goes?" I ask him, all business.

"Sure, great." He turns eyes to the screen. "Okay. Question One: *On Monday, the minimum temperature in Mathville was -11°C and the maximum temperature was 14°C. What was the range of temperatures on Monday in Mathville?* Wow." He looks over at me, one eyebrow raised. "I had no idea there was a place called Mathville. Who makes these up?" Then he frowns at the screen. "Okay, range of temperatures."

"I know, eh?" I say and bite my lip so I don't just blurt out the answer.

18. RESEARCH

I'm searching the Internet for information about Magnus Haugen.

Why? I don't know. I just am. Sydney planted this seed and it's sprouting, what can I say? I'm curious.

I have no idea what I'll do with any information about her Viking boyfriend (is that even the right word?), if I find it. Maybe I'll understand Sydney better. Maybe she'll want to talk about him and I'll be able to picture him as she unloads.

Maybe I'm just seeing a problem that needs to be solved.

So, I don't know the spelling, but typing "magnus howgen curling" into Google works like magic. *Did you mean Magnus Haugen curling* responds the invisible search magician, and suddenly, my screen fills with images and links to click on.

I thought he'd be blond. Aren't all Scandinavians blond? No, they're not. This guy has a round face, high cheekbones, and slightly slanted eyes. Heavy eyebrows. A lot of dark brown hair, flopping to one side. He's tall, too. There's a photo of him during a curling game, standing beside another shorter guy, both of them leaning on their brooms (yes, thanks to my dad, I know my curling equipment terminology). Red jackets with blue and white. In this photo, they're wearing typical black pants, but in another one, I see him sliding out with a curling rock in front of him, and he's wearing bright red-and-blue-checked pants. Fancy.

Magnus Haugen, Norwegian curler, says one of the links, so I click on it and read through some random biographical details. Born in Bergen, seventeen years old. Plays third. National junior champion, twice. Youth Olympics team, playing third. Scores, teammates, events. All fairly uninteresting.

I click on a YouTube link, and suddenly Magnus Haugen is in action, leaning over with a broom out in front of him, and he's gazing intently down the sheet of ice. A couple of Swedish (I think—blue and yellow, three crowns on their jackets?) boys stand behind him, looking nervous. There's a voice doing commentary: "And it comes down to the last shot of the tenth end for the win. Haugen holding the broom. Nilsen gets set to throw ..." The camera switches to the other end of the ice, and another Norwegian player slides out with a rock and the camera follows it down the ice, two other players there sweeping the ice like crazy. It's a beauty. Rocks go flying, brooms in the air, much hugging, sad Swedish boys, handshakes, more hugging and yelling. *Norway's Torger Nilsen wins World Juniors.* Last year.

They hung out at a curling camp in Switzerland, Sydney said. I scroll through more photos to see if I can find anything. Some reference to Switzerland, to curling camps ...

And then, suddenly, there's a photo and story from just a few weeks ago. An event in Sweden and a photo—that has to be him, right? Those eyes, that floppy hair—of Magnus Haugen and a small group, guys and girls dressed up as if it's a party, maybe a closing banquet. He's next to a blonde girl who's laughing at the camera and he has his arm around her, their heads close together. Snuggled, you might say. *Norway's Magnus Haugen, Torger Nilsen, Sweden's Annalise Karre, and Switzerland's Katrina Schulz enjoying the after-party at the Karlstadt Junior Curling Invitational.*

Oh, dear. I wonder if Sydney has seen this?

Of course she's seen this. If I, a complete stranger to these people and this sport, can google Magnus Haugen and find my way to this photo, then she can and probably has, too.

I zoom in. He's good-looking, all right. Tall and strong, a definite Viking vibe, even if his hair isn't blond. Annalise is good-looking, too, and the way they're pressed together pretty well screams, "Couple!"

I stare at the laptop screen for a few minutes longer, then shut it with a click.

But that doesn't shut it all away. Sydney wants to tell him about the bump she's currently carrying around inside her. I wonder what she thinks this will accomplish. Will it make her feel better? Does she think he will even want to know? Will he be happy and offer to marry her and raise their child in a happy home down the street from the curling club? Will he ignore her? Say nasty things about her? Deny that it even happened?

I'm looking too far ahead, I know. It's what I do, despite my mother's constant reminders about *the rule* ... But Sydney's voice fills my head.

I haven't told him—yet.

I really, really wish she hadn't told me.

19. MEET THE PARENTS

The Help Desk has been amazingly busy this afternoon for some reason, which is a good thing, because it keeps me from thinking too much about the moment when Finn Nordin will come walking through the door of String Theory, look around, see me sitting there with some needy knitter with needles and yarn clutched in their hands, and say, "Hi, Bliss. I'm here to work on math problems with you."

Well, no, I don't actually expect him to say that, but there will be an entrance, and people, especially my parents, will be sure to notice.

It's not that men don't come to String Theory. We have many male regulars—Knit & Natter's Oscar, for instance. And a bunch of guys from the local Artisans Collective. And, of course, Dad is around most of the time. Anderson is a regular, too.

But mostly when a teenage boy walks into our store, he's

trailing behind a girlfriend. Or, on rare occasions, usually around Christmas, a mother.

So, while I'm tinking Mrs. Calabrese's afghan project—Fun Fact: "tinking" is basically knitting backwards to reach and correct a mistake. *Tink. Knit.* Get it?—I keep my eyes on the task and try not to glance up too nervously whenever the door opens.

And the door is opening a lot. We are so busy today. Mom and Dad are in constant conversation, taking turns coming out from behind the front desk to help people find the best yarn for baby blankets (soft, but it also has to be machine washable), dishcloths (cotton, self-striping), and warm sweaters (bulky or worsted weight, maybe some acrylic in with that wool). Someone has questions about knitting in the round. Someone wants to know about the classes, the Knit & Natter, the kits for making adorable monkeys (freaky horror-movie monkeys, if you ask me) and Hudson Bay blankets.

It's a circus. Three rings going constantly. So, I'm actually head down over a messed-up row of bobbles and cables—"I was watching one of those home renovation shows, Bliss, and just not paying attention"—when I realize that he's there.

"Okay, Mrs. Calabrese, I think that's got it," I say, giving Mrs. Calabrese her blanket and catching a glimpse of backpack, hockey jacket, tall someone—Finn, standing there, smiling at me deep in Help Desk action.

"Cool," he nods. "Hi, Bliss. Hope I'm not late."

Mrs. Calabrese is one of our regulars, a quiet, well-dressed senior who took up knitting late in life (she told me on her first visit to the Help Desk), when she retired from head office at some big insurance company and decided she needed projects to work on that still involved numbers but didn't require dealing with people.

"She's all yours," she says to Finn, while she stows her knitting into her bag and packs up to leave. "I'll get out of your way so you and your friend can talk, Bliss."

Finn smiles. Smiles charmingly. She winks at me over her shoulder.

Oh, God. Adults.

"Bye, Mrs. Calabrese." I wave her away, all cool and composed, before glancing up at Finn. "Hi. No, you're not late. Grab a chair."

He's still standing, though, taking it all in.

As someone who sees it every day, I forget that the String Theory space can be overwhelming, with its blocks of colours, and the mish-mash layers of shelves, and the displays of completed knitted projects. Books, needles, notions, and, always playing in the background, Dad's playlist, which can be anything from classical to Disney to 80s hits to boy bands. Today, it's Rachel Portman soundtracks, currently at *Emma*. I'm so used to it, I forget that it might take a minute to process.

"Is it okay?" he says. "I mean, I'm not interrupting? You look busy."

"No, I'm done." Mrs. Calabrese is now over at the cash, talking to Dad. I see them both turn and look at us. "If someone else comes in, I'll have to take a break, but this is good timing, actually. Sit. Really. It's good."

"Help Desk. That's great." He takes his jacket off and drapes it over the back of the chair, pulls his laptop out, gets settled in.

"Hi, you must be Finn." My mother appears at the table. "Bliss told us you were coming in to do some math contest prep today. I'm Rowan, very nice to meet you." She sticks out her hand and they shake.

"Hi, Mrs.—uh—Rowan," he sort of laughs.

"First time to String Theory?"

Oh, Mom. Come on. We had this conversation already at the dinner table when I told you he'd be coming in. Please, just smile and leave, okay?

"It is, yes. Great store. I love the name."

"He loves the name of the store, Patrick," she calls over to Dad, who has just said goodbye to Mrs. Calabrese and has a moment to lean on the counter and check in on us.

"Of course he does. Math people get it, right?" Dad laughs, and then waves a greeting. "Hi, Finn. Nice to meet you."

Okay, so now poor Finn has met my parents and, sort of,

Mrs. Calabrese. I'm squirming with embarrassment. *Can we just get on with our contest prep, please, people?*

"Hi, Mr. Adair."

"Pat, please."

"Pat." He laughs and shakes his head. "Sorry, my parents would freak out if my friends called them by their first names."

"Well, we're old, so we don't care," shrugs Dad.

I have a weird moment when I realize that I've been calling his mother Lauren in my head now for a few weeks. I'd better not ever, ever say that out loud.

"My mom comes here on Wednesday nights for the thing, the group thing?"

Mom jumps on it, of course.

"Our Knit & Natter! What's her name?"

"Lauren Nordin," he says, and they both smile delightedly at each other, completely unaware of the loud boom of all the pieces falling into place.

"Lauren! Of course." Mom beams at him. "You look a lot like your mom."

"Everybody tells me that."

They laugh, a moment shared between this nice boy and my mother. This is getting more and more uncomfortable for me and I don't know why. Actually, I do. Dark hallway, overheard conversation that neither of them have a clue about. Just me ...

99

"Yeah, and it must be my mom's influence, cause some friends and I joined Bliss's knitting club thing at school, too."

"Excellent!" Mom is in heaven. Doing good works is her thing. Doing good works that involve yarn—and me—is even better. This all shows on her face. I think she might be ready to invite him to Sunday dinner.

It's true, though. Finn, Karlee, and Adele did, in fact, show up at 3C Club on Thursday and, as I wandered the room, helping the other knitters and checking in with Sydney, I watched as Anderson and Charis got them started on the K2 P2 scarf. Actually, Karlee started with a straight garter stitch knit-knit-knit scarf. She doesn't seem to have much fine motor skill prowess, but the yarn she chose (a fuzzy acrylic in a gorgeous shade of lilac) was perfect, so she's not without artistic vision, I believe. She just smiled when they were leaving and Finn called out to me, "See you Saturday, Bliss." Adele just ignored everyone.

Finn and my mom are still having a moment here on Saturday afternoon, though.

"Actually, my little sister is interested in the kids' program you have here, too." Finn swivels between Mom and me now. "Mom said it was kind of an independent thing, but you could get her started. Beginner stuff, you know?"

"Talk to Bliss," says Mom. "She's your girl." *So, so awkward,*

Mom. But Finn doesn't seem to notice her choice of words, even if I see Dad over at the counter grinning madly.

"Okay." Finn turns back to me, nodding. "Maybe when we're done, you can fill me in on what we have to do. Mom can bring her in, or I can. Whatever."

"Of course, no problem."

"Great. Ava will love that."

"Great."

Okay, surely it's time for math, right? And my mother must be a mind reader, because ...

"Okay, you guys, I'll get out of the way and you can have fun," she says as she moves away, back to work. "Ha. Fun with math. Not my department, I'm afraid."

"Nope, all mine," says Dad. "And Bliss's, of course."

The two of them are now standing over at the front desk, beaming at us.

So embarrassing. But Finn just grins and doesn't even seem to notice. He turns back to me and opens his laptop, searches for the documents he needs.

"Your parents are cool," he says, and because two shoppers just came out of the fingering/sock yarn aisle and are now piling skeins on the counter and asking about needles, my cool parents turn their attention away from us, so they don't hear him.

A sigh of relief escapes me.

"What?" he asks.

"Oh, nothing." I wave that moment of relief away. Raise my eyebrows meaningfully. "Just ... parents. You know."

"Yeah." His eyes are on his screen. "Parents."

His voice, just for that word, sounds different. I glance over at him and can't help noticing that little scar beside one of his eyes. His very blue eyes. His long fingers resting on the keyboard as he gazes at the screen. I wonder if he plays piano. Or guitar. He seems like someone who would be good at music. I wonder why he said "Parents" like that ...

"So, have you got the practice questions up?" he says, sounding normal again. Upbeat. Ready to have fun with math. I drop my eyes before he can look over and catch me watching him. "Where do you want to start?"

Good, okay, we're back to math. I try to ignore my parents who are over at the front desk being busy and professional, while clearly enjoying the sight of their little Bliss over at the Help Desk with this nice boy, Finn.

"Have you looked at the questions from two years ago?" I ask, all business. "They're pretty tricky."

"Good, let's start there," he says, and we're off, deep into Math Question Heaven, which apparently suits us both.

Yeah. Parents.

20. THE KNITTING CURE

On Sunday, Auntie Bryn comes over for supper again. In the summer, we don't see so much of her on weekends because she takes off with various friends and colleagues from the college and attends festivals and does camping trips. Mom and Dad keep hoping she'll come back from one of these adventures and announce that she's found love again.

It never happens. I think Auntie Bryn found love, and lost it when Stefan died, and is not interested in finding it again because no man can measure up to Stefan.

"This is bliss, Bliss," she says, all dreamy, eyes closed, as we sit together in the family room by the fireplace.

She's at one end of the couch and I'm at the other. Our feet and legs are kind of tangled up in the middle, under a blanket knitted by my great-grandmother Molly. (Yes, knitting is a family trait or trademark or addiction, whatever.) It's nothing fancy, just row after row of garter stitch. But Granny Molly knitted it with two strands of fat, soft, textured wool that drifts in and out of shades of blue and purple. It weighs a ton. The only way to wash it is outside with a hose in summer, and then it has to be left to dry on the picnic table.

Now, mid-winter, when it's cold and you just want to stay inside and hibernate, Granny Molly's blanket is perfect. Its weight holds you down, warm and safe. When I was little, I would sometimes drag it upstairs to my bedroom, spread it out on the floor, crawl under it, and feel invisible in the best, coziest way.

So, Auntie Bryn and I are curled up on our ends of the couch under Granny Molly's blanket. Mom and Dad are in the kitchen making pasta and garlic bread and salad for our supper. I hear vegetables being chopped, the clunk-clink of utensils, low conversation, the occasional shared laugh.

"More wine, my darling?"

"Thanks, love."

My parents are like a Hallmark movie. Sometimes it's just safer to stay out in the family room with Auntie Bryn, who is simply parked here, sharing couch and blanket with me, eyes closed, hands wrapped around a big mug of hot chocolate and Baileys.

When she says that about bliss, I look up, but her eyes are closed and I know she doesn't expect an answer. Which is fine, because I'm not in an answering mood right now.

I'm actually in a weird place.

Yeah. Parents. I'm in that place, with Finn Nordin, sitting at the Help Desk. His mother is in my weird place, too. The woman in the red coat, talking on her phone. Her voice in the hallway.

And I'm also on the bench by the river with Sydney, talking about Magnus Haugen, who is hovering in the background with his arm around some cute Swedish curling girl named Annalise.

So, I'm doing what I always do when I find myself in weird places in my head—I knit.

It's the simplest of all patterns, a baby blanket knit on the diagonal. Mindless, but so satisfying with its line of eyelet around the border, and the soft, variegated yarn that drifts from one pastel to the next without any effort. With mindless, minimal effort, I can produce this sweet, cozy blanket for someone's baby.

Which brings me back to Sydney. The next time I see her (and her baby bump), I will be seeing Magnus Haugen standing there, too. And because I have a very precise and vivid imagination, I will see her and Magnus standing close together—no Annalise in sight—and I will see them laughing on the curling ice, and walking around that place in Switzerland, and sitting in the team van, and—what did she call it?—bonding.

Knit three, yarn over, knit to end of row.

I would like not to be thinking about bonding, but Sydney and her situation has found its way into my head and my head is like a trap. I remember everything she said. Words conjure up images, and there we go.

Bonding.

Which brings me to the other images floating around in my head: Finn Nordin's mother standing outside String Theory, smirking into a phone. Talking to The Young Guy? Or to the friend she called in the dark hallway? Thinking about Finn's mother makes me think of Finn's long fingers on his laptop keyboard, and the way he grins when we get the answer right. That little scar beside his eye. Where did that come from? A hockey puck? A fall from his bike when he was little? (He must have been an adorable little boy ...)

Knit three, yarn over, knit to end of row.

Finn and Karlee. I wonder if they, um, bond?

Stop it, Bliss!

I knit another row, another row, another row, counting every stitch and trying to clear my mind so that the only thing I know is the slide of the needle into the loop, the swish of the yarn over the joined needles, slipping the base loop off. And one more. One more.

The knitting cure.

"Goodness," says Auntie Bryn.

I glance up at her and see her watching me with an expression of concern on her face.

"You okay?" she asks.

"Yup. Fine."

Knit three, yarn over, knit to end of row.

"Your lips are moving," she says.

"Counting stitches."

"Right." She doesn't believe me. Takes a sip of her hot chocolate.

I knit some more, feel the rhythm. Feel Auntie Bryn's feet snuggled against mine under Granny Molly's blanket. Hear my parents laughing about something in the kitchen.

"You can always talk to me, you know that, don't you, Bliss?" Her voice is quiet, just for me.

"I know. Thanks, Auntie Bryn."

She sighs. I knit.

21. FIRST GAME: PREGAME

The senior boys volleyball team has its first game on Tuesday and I'm twitching with nerves.

"What have you got to be nervous about?" Anderson asks at lunch, while doing a number on a tomato and avocado pita sandwich. "I'm the one who might actually get off the bench and have to perform in front of people. You know, for points."

He's grinning through the sauce that just can't help sliding down his chin.

I hand him a napkin and he wipes but he doesn't stop chewing and grinning.

"I don't know. I just want you to have fun," I say. I chew daintily on an apple slice in an effort to model good eating behaviour. "To do well, of course, and I know you will. But have fun, too."

"Thanks, Mom," he says through another mouthful, and I realize he's exactly right, because I am going to be the Mom At

The Window this afternoon.

"Ready, Andy?" Bethany appears and plops down across from me. She is probably the only person who calls him this, and I hate it.

"Anderson is a perfectly good name, Bethany. You should use it."

They shake their heads at each other. *Oh, Bliss. Here we go. Again.*

"So, why is your first name a last name?" she asks him.

"Maybe for the same reason Bliss's first name is an old-fashioned word for happiness that nobody uses anymore?"

Oh, we're on fire today. Maybe this is Anderson's technique for warming up.

James comes by with a tray stacked with today's offering—macaroni and cheese. It looks hideous—all slimy cheese and sketchy breadcrumbs on top—but I've noticed people don't seem to notice these details. I wonder if this is a boy thing. Or maybe just a hunger thing ...?

"Hey, guys, got room?"

"Sure, join us," says Anderson. "I'm just getting grief over my fascinating first name."

"You have an excellent first name and don't let anyone tell you otherwise," James says as he settles himself across from Bethany. "Hans Christian was an Andersen, right?"

"Yes, but ..." Bethany is about to protest that's a last name, of course.

"Mrs." I say.

"The best." James says what we're all thinking.

Mrs. Anderson really was the best. Our kindergarten teacher, the year Anderson, James, Bethany, and I met. She was kind, funny, and could do card tricks. She also had a voice like an opera singer and would launch into full *bel canto* during the "Tidy Up" song after playtime.

"She got me," Anderson says.

"She got all of us," says James.

The four of us nod in agreement on that one. Mrs. Anderson knew that Bethany needed to be part of every conversation, every school event, so she gave her a badge and made her Class Social Monitor. She asked James, whose parents didn't speak English very well, to teach us useful words in Urdu so we could say hello and thank-you to them on Parents Night. And Anderson, with his stoic ability to ignore the "Hey, Fatso!" taunts on the playground—she drew him out of his shell by having him show us all how far he could kick the soccer ball. (Far! And then she sent mean-mouthed Peter all the way down the field to retrieve it. Brilliant.)

And me. She got me, too. Me and my pages of graph paper, with little numbers written in each square, that I brought for

Show and Tell. "Bliss, one day you and your love of numbers are going to make a difference in the world," she told me as my classmates stared at my papers in total incomprehension. The first knitting project I completed—a scarf, from that bright blue shiny yarn that I chose myself—I gave to Mrs. Anderson.

"Well, whatever," Bethany says. "I'm still going to call you Andy."

Bethany does what Bethany wants to do, and gradually it occurs to me as we all grin at each other, that she and James are grinning at each maybe a bit longer than the rest of us. And then she drops her eyes and—is she *blushing?*

"So, what are my chances of getting off the bench and actually into a game?" Anderson and James launch into a rundown of the other guys on the team, things Coach Coslov said in practice, and volleyball talk that goes right by me because I'm chewing my apple and watching Bethany, who continues to fork up her salad in a ladylike manner and ignore us all. Except she's smiling a little as she ignores us.

James and Bethany? What?

22. THE ANDERSON VARGA FAN CLUB

"This is ridiculous," Bethany mutters a little too loudly.

"Shhh!" I lean into her to make sure she hears me. "Not helping."

"Not helping is what stupid Coslov is doing right now."

Two girls in front of us turn around just enough to identify who we are and exchange a glance with each other. *What's their problem?*

The problem is that Central lost the first game 25–2 and is now well on its way to total defeat, trailing 9–1 in the second game of the best-of-three.

And the bigger problem is that Anderson is still sitting on the bench. He doesn't look upset, or nervous or anything. He's just sitting there, clapping on points scored, watching the action in that calm way he has. I don't know how he does it. I'd be twitching and jumping up and at least jiggling one foot. Not Anderson.

"Might just be a coaching strategy," Sydney, on my other side, says into my ear so that the experts in front of us don't get a chance to react. "You know, stick with a certain rotation for this first series, just to see how the team does."

Which might make sense, except that Anderson is the only player who hasn't seen action yet this afternoon.

A groan from the Central crowd around us in the bleachers—10–1 for Westview.

"I can't watch," Bethany puts her head in her hands and heaves a giant sigh. "So not fair."

Coach Coslov calls a time out.

"Watch," says Sydney, and when I turn to ask her what I'm supposed to be watching, I see that her eyes are on the coach, and she nods at me to look, too. Coach Coslov is bent over, talking to the scrum of players. She's seeing something that I don't see, obviously. "See? See that?"

"See what?" Bethany lifts her head and we both watch the scene over at the Central bench, totally confused. "I see the coach talking to the players, but Anderson ..."

Anderson is tightening his laces, stretching his fingers. Coslov glances over at him, nods. Says something, and Anderson stands up off the bench and joins the scrum.

"Look!" I nudge Bethany. "He's going in!"

He is going into the game. He and Ibraham, the other setter, tap hands, and there's Anderson, walking calmly out onto the floor, taking up his position in the back corner of the court, swinging his arms a little and bouncing on his feet to warm up.

He looks huge and out of place and I'm suddenly terrified for him. I can't help it. I haven't seen Anderson on a volleyball court since middle school, and he's so much bigger now. I feel as if I'm watching my best friend about to make the biggest mistake of his life. Maybe he is. And it would be my fault for bugging him, telling him to sign up. He's going to hate me.

And then someone behind us says: "Wow. Who let the whale out?" And there's laughter around us.

All three of us turn and glare at two Grade 12 guys who clearly couldn't care less that three insignificant Grade 11 girls disapprove, and just as Bethany is saying, "Shut up, jerks," we hear the whistle and Sydney pulls me back around ...

... to see Anderson run smoothly into position, receive a pass on his fingers, and float the ball up high into the air for one of the other players to smash across the net into the floor, which is now littered with Westview players who missed saving it.

Whistle. Score 10–2. Central serve.

The cheers are sudden and shockingly loud. We three join in and even the jerks behind us get into the action. The bleachers rock a little.

On the next point, the ball comes back over the net and is

barely retrieved by James, who gets it in the air, but Anderson still has to run to get under it. And he does, making it look easy. Again, the ball floats up in the air and this time one of the other guys smashes it into the floor.

After one and a half sets of witnessing our team being squashed, the Central crowd is going cautiously berserk. Bethany, Sydney, and I are going just as cautiously berserk as everyone else. It's like someone flipped a switch.

Anderson is killing it, but he makes it look easy, the way he floats around the floor, just moving as much as he needs to. It's as if he can tell where the ball is going before anyone else does. It's magic. I'm clutching Bethany's arm and we're both yelling his name. The girls in front of us are laughing and, it seems, we're all on the same team now.

Another point for Central. Another point. Central ties. Central goes ahead. Central wins the second game, and now the crowd really goes wild as the players jog over to the sideline for another scrum with Coach Coslov.

"Can you believe it?" Bethany is bouncing up and down, taking my arm with her, which is not very comfortable, but I let her because I'm just as excited.

"He is really, really good," Sydney says.

And then, just as the players jog back out to the court and give each other whatever weird ritual taps and slaps they do—

including Anderson, who seems to be the main guy out there now, the one they all need to tap, slap, or bump last before getting into position—we hear the guys behind us, loud enough that their voices carry around our little section in the bleachers.

"I guess the whale can play, eh? Who knew?" Followed by stupid, cool-guy laughter.

A few laughs roll around us in the bleachers, but Bethany and I freeze and turn. As one. I'm afraid of what might come out of her mouth because the look on her face is terrifying, and I bet my face is exactly the same. Her mouth is open, ready to take them on.

Yes, brave Grade 11 girls taking on the jerk Grade 12 boys in the bleachers at a volleyball game. When it comes to defending Anderson, we are fearless.

But before we can say a thing, another voice says, "Shut up, jerks."

Cameron Tellez is in their row, but further down. Cameron and Peter. And while Peter looks as if he wants to hide under the seat, Cameron looks—well, actually, he just looks disgusted, and that's exactly what we all hear in his voice.

People are turning to check it out now because this is almost more exciting than the action on the gym floor. The Grade 12 guys look at each other and laugh.

"Yeah, you jerks, shut up," says one of the girls in front of us.

"Hey," one of the guys raises his hands in front of him, like he's protecting himself. "He's good. That's all I'm saying." He looks down the row at Cameron. "He's good, man. Relax."

We all know backpedalling when we see it.

The game is underway again, and because of our little drama in the bleachers, we've all missed seeing Central go up 2–0. Before I turn back to see Anderson make another perfect set for another smash, and a dig and volley over to our side, and a perfect pass to Anderson, who sets it for another smash into the gym floor and another point—and another round of loud cheers around me—I glance at Cameron, who is back watching the game and looking as if he wants to punch someone. Maybe that Grade 12 guy.

"Go, Anderson!" Bethany yells, and the girls in front of us turn to ask if that's our friend's name.

"Anderson Varga," says Bethany. "He's a volleyball star. His grandfather was in the Olympics."

The girls, suitably impressed, turn back around and yell, "Go, Anderson! Go Central!"

Yes, it's the Anderson Varga Fan Club up here in the bleachers, and everyone is getting on board as the score climbs higher and higher for us. Even the jerk guys behind us are cheering, and the match ends 2–25, 25–10, 15–4 for Central.

Anderson is part of the hand-slapping, hugging, fist-bumping team—although he remains his calm and solid self throughout all these rituals—and just before they head back toward the locker room, he looks up at the bleachers, which are starting to thin out.

Bethany's jumping up and down and yelling at him, "Anderson! Anderson!"

He grins and waves and the three of us wave back. Big crazy waves. He laughs, pauses for a moment, looking at the bleachers, and then heads off toward the celebration in the change room.

Okay, done. But as I turn and follow Bethany along to the stairs, I see Cameron and Peter still standing there in the row behind us. Peter's on his phone, texting, but Cameron is gazing out at the gym floor. He sees me watching and turns away.

"That was nice of you, Cameron," I say. Nod back to where the jerk Grade 12s had been sitting.

"Yeah, well," he says and shrugs. "Come on, let's go." He nudges Peter and they turn and go down the row, down the steps ahead of us.

"That was so exciting!" Bethany can't stop chattering. Sydney is laughing at her, asking why Anderson never tried out for the team before, when he's so good. I let the two of them talk because I'm exhausted. Why am I exhausted?

I think maybe I'm not very good at being The Mom At The Window.

And I also wonder if I should tell Anderson what Cameron did.

118

23. DISTRACTIONS

"Okay, guys, remember how to cast on?" Charis says.

Thursday lunch hour, and Crafting for Community Care Club is underway in Mrs. Badali's classroom. Attendance has been taken, at the insistence of two Grade 12 girls who clearly don't want to miss out on their participation marks. ("I work at the mall," one of them told Charis the first day, "so this is practically the only club I can join that fits my schedule." Nice motivation there but, whatever.)

Sydney is here, already on her second scarf, and that nervous girl, Amanda, has attached herself to Anderson. That would be the famous Anderson Varga, who got a shout-out at assembly on Wednesday morning for his fantastic rookie performance in Central's volleyball victory over Westview and drew loud cheers from the entire school for the first time in his life. He just sat there with the team and looked as chill as he always does.

Also, Finn and Karlee, who arrived on time and are now chatting and laughing as they stumble through Charis's instructions. I wonder if their motivation is also participation points, since I remember Finn saying something about hockey and supervising his sister after school, which limits what activities are available. Karlee—no idea what she's doing. She's a terrible knitter as far as I can see.

Some people are still working on their scarves but, today, Charis is walking everyone through the pattern for baby hats, always in demand and easy to complete quickly.

We're nothing if not efficient, here at Central's 3C Club (which I suppose makes us actually 5C? Stop, Bliss. You're distracted ...).

Yes, I'm distracted.

On Tuesday, I was distracted by Anderson's debut on the volleyball court, which went well. But there was that odd moment with Cameron Tellez that I can't seem to let go of. He was so angry at those stupid boys.

And on Wednesday, I was distracted first by Mr. Wenzik asking Finn and me to stay behind after class for a quick chat about our contest prep—"We worked through one of the previous contest papers on the weekend," Finn reported. "We'll probably do some more this weekend, right, Bliss?"—and second, by my made-up excuse to my mother for not being able to hang out at the store that night. I just wasn't up to any interactions with

Finn's mother at Knit & Natter. Even hiding out in the back room didn't appeal. "Lots of homework," I told her. "Is it okay if I just stay home with Dad tonight?"

Of course it was. Mom just smiled and carried on. But I know my mother, and she knows me. And the idea that we might at some point in the future have a conversation about *why* I don't want to hang around String Theory on Wednesday nights is a distracting thought that keeps images of the dark hallway and the sounds of an overheard conversation in my head. And forces knitting needles into my hands long after she comes home and reports to Dad, downstairs, "Lots of laughs tonight. That Oscar! And I told Lauren what a nice boy her son is ..."

Distracting.

So now it's Thursday, lunch hour, and I'm moving around the room, helping people with their long-tail cast-on.

"Which finger holds the tail?"

"How long is it supposed to be?"

"I'm doing this wrong, aren't I?"

Anderson and I are doing lots of consultation and repair work, but everyone seems to be enjoying themselves, including Finn and Karlee. He's a natural, actually, and picks up the technique right away, but she's hopeless.

"How did you ever learn to play the piano?" he says and she giggles, unwinding yarn from her fingers and making a tangle on the desk. "Hey, Bliss? Can you show Karlee again?"

"Sure." Efficient and business-like, I come over to their desks—pushed together, very sweet—pick up the snarled mess of yarn (gorgeous, soft, pink, shiny baby yarn) and quickly unravel and rewind it onto the ball. "There you go. Just make a loop and estimate the length you need by wrapping the yarn around the needle, right? Do you need me to show you again?"

"Show her?" Finn says, one eyebrow raised. "No, I think you need to bypass *show* and go straight to *do it for her.*"

"You're mean." Karlee laughs and punches him on the arm in a delicate you're-so-cute-I-would-never-hurt-you kind of way.

The cuteness is, yes, distracting, so I just go to work, pulling out a length of yarn, wrapping it around the needle in an estimate of how many stitches need to be cast on, and then quickly pulling the tail through the loops and onto the needle until the first stitches are there, lined up and ready to be transformed (many rows later) into a cute little hat for someone's baby.

"Wow," says Karlee. "You're so fast."

"Hey, she's an expert." Finn grins at me. "You should have seen this crazy mess she fixed for this lady at String Theory on Saturday."

I didn't know how long he had been standing there at the Help Desk, watching me and Mrs. Calabrese's messed-up cable-bobble disaster but, clearly, it was long enough to see part of my rescue.

"That's my job. Fixing things."

"Well, you're good at it," says Finn.

"Help Desk," I shrug. "That's me."

"So, now I do that knit two-purl two thing again?" asks Karlee, with the needles held awkwardly in her hands and her eyes on the pattern sheet that Charis has handed out.

"Like this, right?" Finn demonstrates. His stitches are even and just loose enough for him to slip the needle in easily and slide the finished stitch off when it's done. Maybe it's those long fingers that make it easy for him to hold the needles and feed in the yarn. I don't comment on this, of course. His knitting technique or his long fingers.

I move off to see how other people are doing (mostly badly) but he calls me back.

"Hey, Bliss. Can I bring my little sister to the Help Desk on Saturday? She wants to try knitting, too, you know, now that my mom and I are both getting so good at it." Swagger. Karlee thumps him again and they laugh. Such a cute couple.

"Sure, no problem. Bring her along," I say. "Happy to get her started."

"Great, see you then." He nods and turns his gaze back to his blue-green baby hat and Karlee, who's biting her lip in concentration as she awkwardly loops the yarn around and knits one stitch very, very slowly.

24. GIRLS' NIGHT: PART ONE

On Friday at lunch, Bethany has one of her brilliant ideas.

"Hey! Do you guys want to come over tonight and hang out? Girls' Night?"

"Sure!" Sydney says, almost before Bethany has finished. "What time? What's your address?"

She sounds desperate. I can just imagine what Sydney's Friday nights at home with her grandmother are like. (Not to dis Mrs. Bart—she's lovely. But she is a grandmother, and that comes with a certain level of low expectation, I'm sorry to say.)

"Girls' Night." Hmmm. "What does that mean, exactly?"

Bethany can go in many different directions at any given time, so I've learned it's best to confirm exactly what's going on in her head when she comes up with these fabulous plans for "hanging out." Movie marathons? Mani-pedis and facials? Competitive board games? Yoga and/or workout videos on

YouTube? Sitting around eating popcorn (or some bizarre snack, prepared from a recipe found online), and then going through last year's Central yearbook and commenting on everyone we—mostly she—might know?

I have experienced every one of these activities, so I just want clarification.

"Oh, you know. Eating stuff. Drinking stuff. Talking about stuff. Kicking my brothers out of the rec room and taking over the TV."

"Sounds great," Sydney says with deep feeling and forks up a mouthful of salad. I think I've probably read her home-with-grandmother situation correctly. "Come on, Bliss. You're in, right?"

"What is Bliss in for?" Anderson pulls out the chair next to me, plops down, and we exchange a look. He knows Bethany and her plans as well as I do. "Am I invited?"

"You're always invited." Bethany nods at him. "Hanging out at my house tonight."

"Ah. Maybe not this time," he says, and I clock Sydney's face as she tries to understand why Anderson would be part of our Girls' Night and works it out and smiles at him. He's been watching her and he smiles back. "I have plans."

"Go have fun, then. But you know we'll be talking about you, right?" Bethany. She's honest, at least.

"I know. Bliss will give me a report, won't you, Bliss?"

125

It's how our friendship works: I tell him everything and he knows it.

Well, actually, that's not quite true. I still haven't told him about Cameron sticking up for him so publicly in the bleachers on Tuesday during the game. I should, I know. It was a cool thing for Cameron to do, but … I don't know. I'm still trying to figure it out. The *why*. Cameron Tellez has been Gang of Five forever, and this was not what I would call typical Gang of Five behaviour. A problem yet to be solved. So, no, I haven't mentioned that little item yet.

But he's right that he can count on me to tell him everything … Wait. I haven't told him about the existence of Magnus Haugen, either.

What is happening?

"Of course I will. Every detail," I say.

I walk over to Mrs. Bart's house to pick up Sydney right after supper, bundled up because it's early October at its finest—cold, clear, and still. Sidewalk slick with fallen leaves. The stars are up there, way beyond the streetlights and the bare branches of trees.

"Lovely night for a walk," Mom said as I finished supper and got ready to go out. "Call Dad when you're ready to be picked up, okay?"

We made this arrangement because Mrs. Bart called our

house when Sydney came home with the news that she had suddenly landed a social life and was going out for a wild Friday night with the girls, one of whom was me. Mrs. Bart is not used to the teenage girl social scene, so, of course, she checks in with Mom about expectations.

"Hi, Jeanette. Yes, I heard about the girls' plans." Pause, as she listens, glances at me and smiles. "Yes, it's great." Listens. "Yes, I'm sure they'll be fine walking over to Bethany's house together. Yup. Yes, I know." Grins at me. "No, you don't have to worry about that. Pat is on call to drive them home. You don't have to head out into the cold." Another pause and I can see her sympathetic grin. "Don't worry, we're happy to be the taxi service. All right, then? Bliss will be by to pick her up. Thanks, Jeanette. Yup, thanks. Bye!"

She switches off the phone and grins at me. "Nervous grandmother."

So here we are, Sydney and me, walking along the streets of our neighbourhood toward Girls' Night.

"This is great," she says. "I feel as if I've just been let out of prison."

"Oh, no. Is it that bad?"

"No," she laughs a little. "Not that bad. Grandma is great but, you know. It's not quite like being at home."

"Yeah."

There's a pause then, and I expect her to tell me what being at home is like. But then I remember Mrs. Bart saying something about Sydney's mom, and the reasons for coming here in the first place, and the pause extends into an awkward break in our conversation.

"You're going to love Bethany's rec room." I change the subject, which seems a smart thing to do.

It works. She asks questions. I fill her in on the Blake family's brilliance at collecting things—sports memorabilia, vinyl records, movie posters. The Blake twins, Bethany's younger brothers, who compete in junior motocross all summer. Mr. Blake's job as a tech guy for rock bands, so he's often away from home. Mrs. Blake's job as marketing manager for a big clothing line. It's not surprising that Bethany is so wildly hands-on and social.

Xander, age twelve, lets us in when we ring the doorbell.

"She's downstairs," he says without waiting for any boring social exchange. Right to business. "She kicked us out of the rec room."

"Oh, sorry, Xan," I say as I dump my jacket on the bench in the front hallway and pull my boots off.

"She said it was Girls' Night." His twin, Oliver, appears at the curve in the stairs above us. "She said if we came downstairs, she'd put spiders in our beds."

"I'm sure she wouldn't do that," I say, although I can't be sure. But a little reassurance goes a long way with kids, right?

"My cousin once put a frog in my bed when we were staying at their cottage in the Laurentians one summer," Sydney says. "I thought we were friends, but no. A slimy frog. So, just saying, you can't trust anyone."

The two boys stare at her, trying to decide if she's kidding.

"She's kidding, guys." I don't like the look on their faces. Clearly, their world is shattering a little after that delightful story.

"No, it really happened!"

"What did you do with the frog?" asks Oliver.

"Rescued it. Put it in her bed."

The two boys think about that, look at each other, grin.

"Come on." I push Sydney toward the door to downstairs. I notice that the boys haven't moved and are still grinning, plotting, and planning in that silent twins way they have mastered. This works, because I don't think they even noticed Sydney's bump, which means no explanations will be required.

"We'd better warn Bethany to check her bed before she goes to sleep tonight," Sydney mutters as we head down the stairs to our Girls' Night.

25. GIRLS' NIGHT: PART TWO

"Why is there no nice boy like him at Central?" Bethany points—no, *stabs*—at the screen with a spoon dripping with ice cream. Her words are a little unclear, thanks to a cold blob of Mint Chocolate Chip holding her tongue down.

We're watching a marathon of romcoms featuring a nice girl and a nice boy who have just started exploring the boundaries in their relationship (as our Gym/Health teacher Mrs. Magid would say). They're in a car at the end of a date and the questions are racing around—silently, of course—but basically, all coming to the same point: *Will they or won't they?*

Bethany is annoyed because, of course, the boy on the screen is not only great looking, tall, athletic, smart, and funny, but he's also kind, empathetic, supportive, and respectful.

"There's not a single boy at our school who could even come halfway to being as nice as him."

I find it funny because she sounds so mad.

"It's a movie, Bets." I grin at her, watching her jab her spoon at the screen as if someone is responsible for providing her with an answer.

I notice that Sydney isn't grinning, though. She's curled up in the big chair with an afghan over her, bowl of ice cream resting on her bump.

"Why is there no one like him anywhere?" she says in a voice that gives me the uncomfortable feeling she is thinking of Magnus Haugen over there in Norway. Magnus, maybe cozying up to Annalise right at this moment.

Her eyes are on the screen, so she doesn't see me glance at Bethany, who turns to me, eyebrows raised. *What did THAT mean?*

Of course, since I can't tell her, I go for a deflection.

"Anderson is nice," I say.

"Yeah, but Anderson would never kiss a girl," Bethany reminds me. As if I need reminding.

"He's gay, right?" Sydney looks away from the screen and glances over at Bethany and me, sharing the couch.

"He most definitely is gay," Bethany nods, smiles. I think she loves Anderson almost as much as I do.

"And he's out? Like, everyone knows?"

We both nod, still smiling.

"Cool."

The couple in the car has decided the time is not right for them to proceed further, which is just fine with me. I've seen this movie about five times (always here in the Blakes' rec room with Bethany—she loves this guy Peter), but I'm always relieved when they reach this decision.

"Okay, other than Anderson, there is no one at our school who comes close to being as nice," Bethany sighs.

"What about, I don't know, someone like ... James?"

It's been popping up in my head since that moment at lunch the other day, when James sat with us for the conversation about Mrs. Anderson and the two of them were grinning at each other rather excessively. And there was definitely some blushing going on, too.

"Oh." She pops another glob of ice cream in her mouth and leaves the spoon there, like a soother. "James."

Now Sydney and I exchange a glance, and Sydney is the one with eyebrows raised.

"Yes. James," she says. "Spill. Is there something going on there?"

"Well," she shrugs. "He asked me to the dance."

Okay, I did not see that coming. The Not Halloween Dance is coming up in two weeks. It's called the Not Halloween Dance because it's not a dress-up-in-costumes kind of thing. Just a social event on a Friday night, and everyone goes.

Well, everyone but me. I use String Theory as a good excuse for not hanging out in the noisy gym with the rest of the student population who find it fun to dance. Or stand around in clumps, trying to look cool when not being asked to dance. Since Grade 9, Bethany and Anderson and other friends have gone and danced together in a big group. Although, on one memorable occasion, Mr. McArthur and Mrs. Magid, the gym teachers, jitterbugged (I think it's called) in the middle of the floor and then had to give lessons for the rest of the night. Anderson absolutely killed it and everyone wanted to be his partner.

Or so I heard.

"So, are you going?"

"Yes, but only if you come, too." She looks at me pointedly. "He's friends with Taz, you know."

Taz Fenwick. He of the perfect proportions.

"Well, well, well," Sydney has obviously filed Magnus Haugen away and is now sitting up a bit taller, like she's ready for the game to start. Alert, interested, a bit scary, actually. "And who is Taz Fenwick? Have I met him?"

I suddenly feel a strong urge to pick up needles and yarn, but there are none anywhere near me so I make myself appear interested only in the movie with its school scenes, familiar and undemanding. Doesn't work.

"I'm not sure you have any classes with him," Bethany jumps

in. I can hear her voice getting that reality TV vibe again. "He's new this year. He's that tall guy with the beautiful brown skin and an earring. Short hair, a little frosted on top? Hangs out with James—they play in some cricket league his dad started for kids over at the community centre."

"Cricket. Interesting." Sydney looks at me (I see out of the corner of my eye).

I'm not engaging. I don't like where this is going. I long for my slippery needles and skein of hand-dyed lacey yarn in variegated shades of blue, and that shawl pattern with its long row of complicated stitches and lots of counting—*k3, p1, k2, SM, yo, knit to marker, SM, m1L, k1, (k2tog, yo) 2 times, k1 …*

"And when he walked into our English class on the first day of school, Bliss was struck speechless by his beauty."

"Oh, stop it." I have to defend myself or this is going to get out of control. "It was a purely mathematical observation. Or artistic, maybe. He has nice proportions, that's all. I was admiring his proportions."

"Proportions. Right," Sydney snorts. "Is that what they're calling it these days?"

She and Bethany are giggling out of control and, after a minute, I have to join in because I sound like a recruiter for a modelling agency or something. So, there we are, giggling, wiping ice cream drips off our faces, and giggling some more.

Bethany recovers first because she's on a mission now. I have seen her in this mode before so I'm starting to get really, really nervous.

"Yes, James asked me to the dance, and I said yes."

"Bravo!" Sydney taps her spoon against her bowl.

"But I'm not going unless you come, too, Blissy. James and me and you and Taz. A foursome." She probably realizes this sounds very rude to Sydney and turns to her. "Sorry, I'm sure we could find ..."

"No way," Sydney interrupts. "Don't need a date, thanks. Wait. I'll ask Anderson. We can wow everyone with our moves on the dance floor."

She will, too. I can see it now.

"I don't do large school social events. You know that, Bets."

"Come on. It's just a stupid dance. We'll be together. You know James. And Taz is nice."

"I'm sure he is." And yes, I'm sure he is, but ... "I have to work, anyway. My parents ..."

But Bethany cuts me off. She knows my parents, too.

"They will not mind if you miss a Friday night shift at String Theory because you're going to a dance with a nice boy with good proportions." She and Sydney are giggling again. "I'm calling your aunt. She'll talk you into it."

Oh, God. Yes, Auntie Bryn would be all over this.

"I don't know, Bets."

And then Sydney says:

"If Finn Nordin asked you to the dance, I bet you'd go."

This bizarre comment freezes me for a moment. When did Finn Nordin enter the scene?

"Finn Nordin?" Bethany asks. "I didn't know you—but yes, of course! Math buddies! Who needs good proportions when you can get all romantic over quadratic equations!" Still holding the spoon, she smacks her forehead and sends a few blobs of ice cream flying, including into her hair, but she doesn't notice that.

"He has a girlfriend," I say.

"True," says Bethany. "So you're stuck with Taz, right?"

"Excellent. That's settled." Sydney nods, as if she's just delivered the last line in an argument and her decision is final. "School dance. I'm going to invite Anderson to go with me, and he and I will party together while you four hang out and get everyone talking."

I don't say anything because I feel as if I just got pushed over a cliff and am about to land on—something. Either something soft or something jagged and painful.

But part of me is saying: *This could be okay, right?* Bethany will be there, and James, who is a friend. And Anderson and Sydney. And the unknown Taz, who must be okay if he's a friend of James's. And this is what kids do, right? This is what Auntie Bryn has been teasing me about in her kind way—*How's your love life?* She doesn't mean me in a car with a boy, setting boundaries. She means her and Stefan, and finding someone who understands me, and who I can trust and have fun with.

It's The First Rule of Knitting approach again.

"Fine," I say, closing a door in my mind so that I can't see too far ahead. "Okay. I'll go with you guys. And Taz, I guess. If he wants to."

"Yay! Of course Taz will want to go with you!" Bethany starts chattering about what we'll wear, and she's going to text James right now and tell him, and it's going to be great, and Sydney should let Anderson know, too.

And Sydney joins in with questions about what people wear, and can we go together. Will somebody drive us, or what?

I just shake my head—*Oh, you guys are so funny!*—and keep my eyes on the movie, but not seeing it. That closed door in my head is squeaking open, and I see the gym, decorated for the dance, lights turned down. Hearing the music. Me and Taz and Bethany and James and Anderson and Sydney. Dancing. I don't usually dance in public, but maybe I'll be dancing ...

And over there, just in the corner of my eye, for some annoying reason beyond my control, Finn and Karlee keep drifting into sight.

26. AVA

It takes me less than five minutes to realize that Ava Nordin is my kind of girl.

I don't see them come in because I'm head down with a crochet hook, retrieving a dropped stitch about twelve rows back on Carole's baby blanket. Carole only knows garter stitch, thank goodness, so this is not rocket science, but it still takes a delicate, repetitive, orderly series of *hook-loop-pull-through* to calm Carole's agitation and reassure her that the blanket for her niece is going to be just fine.

"You're a magician, Bliss," she sighs.

This is not magic. It's simple yarn and stitch behaviour, but that's okay. Carole had been so mad at herself when she burst through the door of String Theory that Mom instantly jumped out from behind the counter to lead her over to the Help Desk.

"I don't how it happened, Rowan. I just feel so stupid."

Carole is shaking her head at herself.

"It's so easy to drop a stitch and not notice, Carole," Mom reassures her. "You are not the first, believe me. Right, Bliss?" She gives me the *Say the right thing* look.

"We all do it, Carole," I say. "No kidding, it's probably the thing I fix the most, even in my own knitting."

Mom nods. Right thing said. Carole is a lawyer at some big firm in Toronto. She knits on the commuter train to and from the city to keep her mind off work. I can see how distractions might arise if you don't quite succeed at focusing on yarn and needles instead of complicated legal details. I hope she's calmer than this in the courtroom, however.

"Really?" Carole plops down in the chair and pulls the unfinished blanket out of her knitting bag. "Here it is. I put a stitch holder in the loop so it wouldn't unravel further. See?"

"Smart," I say, and mean it. That's helpful, and when I nod at her, Carole smiles.

"Well, at least I did something right." She laughs a breathy little sigh of relief. "I'll watch closely and see if I can figure this out for next time because I'm sure there's going to be a next time."

So, I'm head down, intent on stitch recovery, when the front door opens, and I don't even look up at the people who come in until I hear Mom.

"Well, hello, Finn. And who's this?"

Finn. I freeze the hook in place so I don't do any more damage and glance up quickly.

Finn and a little girl, maybe nine or ten? Barely as tall as his shoulder, wearing a puffy parka with a not-hand-knit slouchy hat. A serious look on her face as she glances around, taking in the unexpected colours, shapes, and lines of the store before turning back to look at my mother.

"Hi, Mrs. Adair. I mean, Rowan. This is my sister, Ava."

"Hello, Ava."

"Hi." A tentative, little-girl voice. Shy?

It would be rude not to look up and notice them, of course, so I pause again. Actually, I'm already on pause, too focused on what's happening at the counter. A moment ago, Carole took a break from following my repair job and she's now up and looking at a new yarn display, so she hasn't noticed my lack of progress.

Finn glances my way, sees me looking. "Hey, Bliss." Waves.

"Hi." I can't wave—my hands are both in use—but I smile at him, and at her. She's not a smiler, I can see. Something I understand. At her age, I wasn't much of a smiler, either.

"Come meet Bliss." He leads the way as my mom tilts her head behind them ("Oh, so cute! What a nice big brother!").

"Ava, this is Bliss. She's the knitting person I told you about."

Ava and I look at each other, and because she's not a big

smiler, I am happy to summon my ten-year-old self and not offer much of a smile back.

"And the math person," she says. "The knitting and math person." She glances up at her brother. "Right?"

"Right," Finn grins. "Knitting and math. That's Bliss."

Yes, it is. Bliss. Both proper noun and regular noun, and as Ava and I look at each other in awkward greeting, I have the distinct feeling she's hearing exactly what I hear.

"I like math, too," she says. "Finn and Mom say I'll love knitting. But I'm not sure yet."

I feel a smile spread just to the corner of my mouth, and see the same smile creeping up on her mouth, too. I love this kid.

"Well, you've come to the right place, then," laughs my mom from over at the counter.

"String Theory," says Finn. "Isn't that great, Ava? Get it?"

Ava Nordin and I exchange a half-smile for another second or so because, clearly, she gets it, and then she says, "I like it here."

Mom laughs. "Well, that's exactly what we like to hear."

"I love it here," calls out Carole, from over at the hand-dyed alpaca display.

"Me, too!" comes the disembodied voice of some other shopper from up the sock yarn aisle.

"Me, too, actually," says Finn, looking down at his sister and then grinning at me, the math and knitting person he has obviously talked about at home. "And this is where Mom comes for her knitting thing on Wednesday nights."

"Oh." Ava nods, thinking about that while I try not to think about dark hallways and overheard private phone conversations.

"So, Bliss could teach you how to knit, if you want."

"Okay." And then she outright smiles at me. "I'd like to learn something new."

Oh, yes, I love this kid.

"Okay, I have to finish this"—I hold up Carole's nearly rescued baby blanket—"and then I can show you, if you want. If you have time?" I glance up at Finn.

"We've got about half an hour before we have to meet up with our mom at the library. Is that enough time?" he asks me.

"Sure, we can get a lot done in half an hour. Just let me finish this and we'll get started."

Ava is pulling something out of her coat pocket—a little wallet.

"I have money to buy what I need," she says, looking at me. "For knitting."

This is absolutely too cute, and I can't help exchanging a look with Finn, who obviously finds this pretty cute, too.

"Why don't you come over here, Ava?" Mom steps out from around the counter. "I'll help you get some needles and yarn, and as soon as Bliss is done, you can get started."

We both know that Mom could just as easily show Ava the first steps of knitting, but she also knows it would be way more fun for Ava if she sits at the Help Desk with Finn and me. She winks at me and leads Ava to the needles display.

"Now, I have some needles that would be just right for you, Ava. They're the same ones I used when I taught Bliss."

Finn watches them go and then turns back to me.

"I know you can't tell, but she's really excited about this," he says, quietly enough that Ava won't hear.

I don't look up at him—focused on the crucial final steps of rescuing Carole's blanket—but I nod.

"I know." And I do.

"So, hey, contest prep. Not today, obviously, but I'm free after school on Monday. Does that work for you?"

The final loop is almost in place—a complicated assembly of stitches, needle, crochet hook, and careful manipulation of all three—so I just nod quickly.

"How about across the street, at the café? We can walk over from school together, if that works for you."

Almost there, sliding another stitch into position ... I nod. "Sure."

Done.

Wait, did Finn Nordin just suggest walking together from school to The Beanbag Café? (Yes, cute name, incorporating

143

both coffee and tea. Get it? And yes, they have squishy beanbag chairs, too, in among the tables.)

And did I just say yes to that?

"Oh, that's fantastic, Bliss!"

I look up just as Carole arrives back at the Help Desk, peering closely at her rescued blanket, and Mom comes toward us with Ava, who's holding needles and a skein of soft, thick, easy-to-handle yarn in her hands.

"All set, Bliss. Ready to turn Ava into a knitter."

"Great," says Finn.

But I'm not sure if he's referring to his sister becoming a knitter, or me agreeing to walk over to the café with him after school on Monday.

A lot is happening here.

"There you go, Carole," I say, and she thanks me loudly, a couple of times, before turning to chat with Mom and heading over to the counter with the blanket safely back in its bag.

Next.

"Okay, Ava, let's get started. You can sit here, and let's get the needles out of their package."

Finn sits beside her and watches her struggle with the cardboard packaging. I'm just about to reach in ...

"Here." Big brother to the rescue.

Next.

"Okay, so Monday after school, right?" I say, not looking at him as I pull out the first strand of yarn for Ava to cast on.

"Yeah. At the café. Or we could do it in the library again. Or here," he looks around. "I was just thinking, it's nice to get out of the school. Go somewhere, I don't know, different."

Somewhere Karlee and Adele won't find us, maybe. Or Bethany and Anderson, or Sydney. Or Taz Fenwick, who (Bethany texted me earlier today) is totally in for the Not Halloween Dance foursome.

"Sure, great." I don't look at him.

But I do look at Ava, who has the same blue eyes as her brother, and who is holding the needles and watching me, waiting for me to teach her how to create something from yarn looped around a needle.

"Okay, Ava. First, you're going to take the yarn like this and the needle like this."

Next. One stitch at a time.

27. SUNDAY CONVERSATIONS

Text from Bethany Sunday morning while I'm sitting on my bed, knitting a shawl with my favourite 3.75mm needles, a sweetly variegated No. 3 yarn and a soothing ten-row-repeat lace pattern. I should be doing English homework (Macbeth: a vocabulary exercise involving unusual Shakespearean words: *minion, cleave, harbinger ...*), but I'm not. I couldn't sleep last night, thinking about what happens when you go along with your friends' brilliant idea at a Girls' Night and get home wishing you hadn't gone along with your friends' brilliant idea.

James says Taz is in. Can I send him your #?

Who's him? I guess she means James, so he can share my number with Taz, maybe? And do I want either of them having my phone number? I text back:

No I'll see him at school

Bethany doesn't push it. The only people who have my number

are her, Anderson, Sydney (and I only shared it with her after our badminton victory, partly because I know Mrs. Bart would like me to), my parents, and Auntie Bryn. That's it. Six people.

I just don't know that many people who I want to text with, and Taz Fenwick is not yet on the list.

Bethany lets it go.

K. Gonna be fun!!!!

Sydney texts a minute later:

So I hear dance thing is ON!!!

I hate to think of the messages that might be flying between her and Bethany.

Apparently

I add the shrugging-girl emoji just to make my point. She must have the fastest thumbs in the world, because it takes her only three seconds to reply:

Nobody texts long words like APPARENTLY just say YASSSS!

Now I'm certain Sydney and Bethany are busy texting each other. I'm sure I can hear them talking about me through the blank space on my message app. Also, who uses the term "YASSSS"? Maybe someone who has travelled the world competing in sporting events and bonding in team vans?

The question now is when I'm going to hear from ...

"Bliss?" Mom calls up the stairs. "Anderson is here."

I didn't even hear the front door, I was so intent on fending off Sydney and Bethany, so wrapped up in this sweet yarn and the click of my needles.

"Come on up!" I yell, loud enough that they can hear me through the closed bedroom door.

Muted words, Mom's laugh, Anderson's steps on the carpeted stairs, the doorknob turning, and there he is, peering at me around the door.

We grin at each other.

"Bliss. What have you gotten us into?"

"Blame Bethany." I look down and keep knitting. Shrug.

Anderson takes up his position on the end of my bed (which creaks) and leans against the wall. We've sat like this many, many times. Me curled up with my pillows stuffed behind me; him leaning against the wall with his legs stretched out in front of him. Talking about stuff. Good stuff. Bad stuff. I'm not quite sure where this conversation is going to land.

"Sydney seems to think I'm going to be her date." When I glance up, he raises an eyebrow at me.

"Relax. She just wants a dancing partner and, of course, we all know you're the best."

"True. Also, I hear ..." Long pause. I knit another few stitches and glance up at him.

"You have a dancing partner, too."

"All Bethany," I insist.

"Taz Fenwick. I never saw that coming."

"Me neither."

"I guess he's kind of cute. Those frosted tips are intriguing."

I shrug, so nonchalant. "I guess."

And then we're giggling together, because he knows that I know he knows what a big deal this is for me. Bliss stepping out. In public at school. With a boy who isn't Anderson.

"Just wait until Auntie Bryn hears," I say. "She's going to go crazy."

That starts the giggles again, and the bed shakes so much under Anderson's weight that it's like being on a car ride down a bumpy road.

But eventually we both settle down, and the only sound is the click of my needles.

"It'll be fun," he says and reaches out to pat my foot, the way you might pat a dog.

"Will it? Will it be fun, Anderson?"

"It will."

"Promise?" I look at him then, and he grins at me. Rests his hand on my foot.

"Promise."

My knight, my protector. My best friend.

My mom calls up the stairs:

"Bliss! Bryn's here! Does Anderson want to stay for lunch?"

We look at each other in mock terror and collapse into laughter.

"Yes, Anderson wants to stay for lunch!" I manage to yell. Then, quietly, to Anderson, "Here we go."

But I'm surprised when Auntie Bryn—"Hello, Gorgeous," as she disappears into a massive hug with Anderson. The adoration is mutual. "Hello, Auntie B."—doesn't mention the whole Not Halloween Dance thing, which I'm not sure Mom would have told her about yet, after a long and weird conversation with my parents on Saturday night, in which I outlined my (My? No, Bethany's) plan for the school dance in a couple of weeks.

No, Auntie Bryn goes right for the other news on the Bliss landscape.

"So, I hear a nice boy and his little sister were hanging out at the Help Desk yesterday. Spill."

Anderson raises an eyebrow at me. Clearly, he's astonished at how much my social circle is expanding these days. I ignore him and give my mother a look. *Really, Mom?*

By now we're pulling out chairs and getting settled for traditional Sunday lunch at the Adair house: tomato soup and grilled cheese sandwiches. Dad's already at String Theory, getting ready for today's one o'clock opening, but Mom has still made double—actually, it may be triple the usual amount. Because, you know, Anderson.

"Finn, the boy that Bliss is doing the math contest with," Mom says, moving around the table and carefully ladling hot soup into our bowls. "You must know him, too, Anderson."

"Ah," says Anderson, face and voice giving nothing away as he takes his first spoonful. "Yes. Finn Nordin." He already has soup dripping down his chin. Honestly. Worst table manners ever.

"Spill," Auntie Bryn says again, waving a hand vaguely at Mom and her soup pot and ladle. "Not you, Rowan. I need to know about Finn Nordin. Who is he?"

"He's a lovely boy," says Mom. She sounds like our grandmother.

Anderson grins at me and politely wipes his chin with his napkin.

"Honestly, you guys, stop it." I reach for a sandwich. "Yes, nice guy. Brought his little sister into the Help Desk because she wanted to learn how to knit."

"Their mother's in Knit & Natter," Mom explains to Auntie Bryn.

"And he and his girlfriend and some female hanger-on are in the Crafting for Community Care Club," Anderson adds, being helpful.

Auntie Bryn sits up straight and looks at me, eyes wide, mouth open, tomato soup dripping back into her bowl from her suspended spoon.

"Who is this paragon? He's nice to his little sister; he's good at math. And he knits!"

I just chew and shake my head. I'm not getting suckered into this conversation. She obviously didn't register the "girlfriend" part.

"Things are picking up." Auntie Bryn lifts her spoon to her mouth, and then splutters soup all over the place when Anderson says:

"And did you hear about Bliss and Taz Fenwick going to the dance together?"

28. A CONVERSATION IS NOT LIKE A KNITTING PATTERN

"Hey, Bliss."

I'm at my locker on Monday morning, somewhere inside a question about geometric sequences from the math contest prep that I was working on before coming to school, so I don't see him coming. Not that seeing him coming would matter. It's not as if I would clock his approach, then nonchalantly close my locker, turn in the other direction, and start walking away from him or anything, although the impulse to do this ripples through me for a nanosecond. Of course, I don't do this. I just turn my head at the sound of a voice.

And there he is, standing beside my locker, smiling at me.

Taz Fenwick. He of the perfect proportions.

"Oh, hi."

He really is a beautiful boy, not just his smooth brown skin and dark eyes (and can anyone tell me why boys always get the best eyelashes?). A hint of black beardy growth on his chin. (Did he not shave or is this a "look"? Anderson would know. I'll have to ask him.) Straight white teeth (braces or good genes?). High cheekbones and eyebrows that almost join in the middle. All in perfect symmetry.

And that's just his face. Then there are the wide (okay, sort of skinny, but wide) shoulders and long arms. His height—I have to look up at him. At him looking down at me.

"So, I guess we're going to the dance together," he says.

"I guess we are." I hear myself and realize that doesn't sound very enthusiastic. *Smile, Bliss.* "Should be fun."

"Yeah."

We stand there smiling at each other for a moment longer, and then, just as I'm thinking, *What do I say next?* and before it gets even more weird than it feels to me already, he glances down the hall behind him.

"Great. Well, see you."

"Okay, see you." Not sure if I'm doing this right, but it sounds like the conversation is over.

He waves one elegant, long-fingered hand (yes, he has elegant hands), turns, and walks away down the hallway.

And that's it. Taz Fenwick and I have just confirmed that we are, actually, going to the Not Halloween Dance together, and—well, and nothing.

Nothing. The boy is beautiful, for sure. Probably nice, too. Who knows? It was a very short conversation.

But nothing really happened. He smiled through it all with no change of facial expression. He didn't stutter or fidget or look nervous (I would find nervousness a bit endearing, I think). No silly small talk about what to wear, or our crazy friends setting us up. And I didn't have anything to add, either, so what does that say about me?

It says that Taz Fenwick and I just had a very dull conversation. A straight garter stitch with not-a-purl-in-sight kind of conversation.

Taz has disappeared down the hall and I'm still watching, but now I'm watching nothing.

But, come on. Straight garter stitch can be good, too, I tell myself. Look at those projects we're doing in 3C Club, right? A starting point. It was a nothing conversation, but a starting point, I tell myself. *Don't look too far ahead ...*

What have I gotten myself into? I go in search of Bethany. I'm sure she'll have an answer.

29. CONVERSATION AT THE BEANBAG

Bethany has no answers. She doesn't know Taz any better than I do, but she thinks it's cute that he came to see me at my locker.

"James told him to do that," she says.

That doesn't help, actually. It means he needs instructions. I hate to think what it's going to be like when we get to the dance and the music starts and we're out on the dance floor. Are Bethany and James going to be shoving us together and saying, *Okay, kids. Now go dance?*

I'm trying not to look too far ahead, but I also feel as if I've been presented with a Level III math contest problem that needs solving, and I don't know where to begin. Maybe the solution is to develop a sore throat the day before the dance, act my way into staying home from school, and offering Taz, James, and Bethany (and Sydney and Anderson) a heartfelt apology for not being able to go? It could work. Pretty sure Anderson would see through it, but he wouldn't say anything ...

"Are you going to the school dance?"

It's like Finn Nordin is inside my head.

I blink a few times to bring myself back to our table in a corner of The Beanbag.

Monday afternoon, after school. Math contest prep up on our laptops, papers spread around in front of us with in-progress solutions. (Also doodles.) His Beanbag mug of coffee. Or maybe it's a latte? I don't speak coffee, so I'm not sure what he ordered. My Beanbag mug of Orange Pekoe. When it comes to tea, I'm not very adventurous.

We met up on the sidewalk in front of the school after last class and walked here. No sign of Karlee or Adele. Anderson has volleyball practice, but a creepy feeling on the back of my neck tells me Bethany and Sydney are somewhere—maybe at the window in the science lab?—watching me walk out to join Finn on the sidewalk. His smile and wave, and his comment about how he's dying for a coffee and his mom will be jealous because The Beanbag has the best, and, *Really? You don't drink coffee?* And how happy Wenzik was when Finn told him we were doing prep today ...

We talk all the way to the café. School stuff, math contest, Ava and her knitting.

"She was so excited about it," he tells me. "She couldn't wait

157

to show Mom. They dropped me at the arena—I had hockey practice—and she was still talking about it."

"Oh, that's adorable. She's so sweet. And smart, too. She picked it up so quickly."

"She's smart, all right," he laughs. I wonder if he's thinking of how Karlee did not pick up knitting that quickly, which is, weirdly, what I'm thinking about.

It's a few long blocks from Central to downtown and the little street of shops where String Theory and The Beanbag sit across from each other. I've done this walk every day since starting Grade 9, and this might have been the fastest ever. Either that, or our conversation created a tesseract and we time-warped there. In any case, we're there, at our corner table, coffee and tea mugs in front of us, laptops open, before I even have time to think about how much conversational territory we covered without even noticing.

And then, after we've cracked open the contest prep and have started looking at a problem involving a large room and how many people can fit into it if everyone is allotted exactly three square metres ...

"Are you going to the school dance?"

The blinking helps me transition from the math problem, through the question: *Where did that come from?* to the solution: *Because we're talking about a lot of people in a large room* to my answer:

"Yes." It takes a lot of work, but I get there eventually. "Are you?"

"Sure. Karlee and Adele wouldn't let me miss a dance." He shrugs. "Not really my scene, but that's okay."

"Not my scene, either," I say and shrug, too.

We're looking at each other with the same expression on our faces. The expression that says, *So, if it's not our scene, why are we going?*

"I guess I'll see you there, then," he sort of laughs. "We can be wallflowers together. Talk about math. And the contest."

This has a certain appeal. Maybe I won't do my sore-throat act after all ...

"... and knitting!" he adds.

"Sounds good to me." And it really, really does.

"It must be great, having this place so close to your store. Are you over here all the time?"

"No, actually, we have a whole tea and coffee set-up at the back of the store, so mostly we just make it there."

There, down the dark hallway, where people have been known to retreat for whispered phone conversations when they think no one can hear them.

"So, I guess we're sitting in the corner here because you didn't want to take one of the window seats and have your mom waving at you the whole time?"

That makes me laugh, because it's so true. When we arrived at the door of The Beanbag a few minutes ago, I glanced across the street and there was Mom, waving and smiling at us from the store window.

"Oh, hi, Mom," I wave back, even though she can't hear me.

Finn waves, too. And laughs, and yells, "Hi, Rowan!" Not sure she can hear, but people on the street certainly do, and I see everyone look toward String Theory. Maybe that was her plan. Oh, Mom.

So yes, a table by the window is completely out of the question, and I lead the way to this table for four in the corner, out of the way, where we can spread out our notes and laptops and focus on the task.

Only it seems we haven't really been focusing on math at all. First, there was the coffee and tea ordering, and waiting for our orders, and then the trip to the condiment table and explaining that yes, I do take cream in my tea, as well as sugar, and I know it's probably unhealthy, but is coffee healthy? Really? And then back to our table and assembling our gear. Laptops, paper, and pens—*Did you get a new mechanical pencil? Cool.*—and, finally, settling down to this question about people, three square metres, and a large room.

So, here we are, at our table in the corner to avoid my waving mother.

"Well, she wouldn't wave the whole time," I say. She wouldn't. But I'm sure she'd be smiling over at us a lot.

He laughs. "Your mother is cool."

"I guess. As mothers go."

It occurs to me that what I just said is really a loaded sentence, and he doesn't even know it. After all, he doesn't know that his mother ...

"My mother's pretty cool, too. I guess."

He's looking at his computer screen like someone who isn't really seeing what they're looking at.

"I haven't met her," I say. This is true.

That snaps him back. "Oh, I thought you might have. She comes to that thing on Wednesday night."

"Knit & Natter. Yeah. I'm not always there for that. My mom runs it."

"Got it," he nods. "She's been going for about four weeks now, I think. She loves it."

Four weeks. I've seen her—or rather, heard her—twice. And then there was the week I stayed home. I'm tempted to ask if Ava takes dancing lessons, but I'm not sure I want to know.

"I was surprised, actually." He glances at me over his laptop. "I mean, you haven't met her, but she sort of has a, I don't know, Pilates, or yoga, or photography vibe. This knitting thing was kind of a surprise to us all."

And then he gets this look on his face as if he just said the most offensive thing ever, so I laugh, because people do this when they think they've hurt my feelings about how uncool knitting is. You know, not as cool as Pilates or yoga or photography.

"Sorry, I didn't mean that knitting ..."

"It's okay," I hold up my hand. "I've heard it before, honestly. I know knitting is cool, so I don't mind what other people think. And besides ..." I point at him. "YOU knit! And your friends, Karlee and Adele. And now Ava. We're all uncool together." Wow. Who would have thought I'd ever include myself in a cool group with Adele?

"Yeah, Adele led us around that clubs thing, looking for the easiest one to get our participation points," he laughs. "She's always looking for the angle."

I can't help myself. "So, let me get this straight. You and Karlee are a couple, and Adele is ...?"

"My cousin."

What? I think my mouth drops open. "Your *cousin?*"

"Yup. My cousin. My dad and her mom are brother and sister. We were born five days apart, so she's practically my twin. Although," he looks off into the distance, head tilted, "I don't think we're anything alike."

You are not anything alike. She's cranky, you're nice. She doesn't like me, you do. I think.

"No, you're not," I manage to say, I hope without giving away what I was just thinking.

"She and Karlee have been best friends since, I don't know, pre-school," he says, math and knitting forgotten, obviously. It's story time. "So, we've always hung out together, and then Karlee and I ..." he shrugs. Grins at me. "Just happened, I guess."

I guess this explains everything, although it doesn't exactly sound romantic. Not like me and Taz and this morning's conversation at my locker, which was, of course, the height of romance.

I look back at my laptop screen and the three-square-metres question. Time to get back to work. Please.

But he's not done.

"If Karlee and I ever break up, I don't think Adele would forgive me." But he laughs when he says it. "She's very protective. No, she's very *territorial* about her friends and family."

Territorial. Good word. Brings up images of wild cats, or polar bears, maybe.

Our conversation seems to have sputtered to a close, which is fine with me. There are too many lines swirling off in different directions, none of which I want to pursue.

"So," he says, sitting up and looking meaningfully at his laptop screen, "How many people can we fit into this big room?"

Math. Math I can deal with.

30. IN A WINDOW

It's dark when we decide we're done. We've covered five questions—worked through them together— and then set some guidelines for collaborating, in preparation for the day of the competition. Well done, us.

Finn snaps his laptop shut and lets out a big breath, as if he's just finished some big task. Which I guess he has. That was a lot of thinking. I'm tired, and I can tell he is, too.

"So, you just go across the street, do you? Meet up with your mom?"

He's shrugging back into a bright blue North Face ski jacket with a ski pass attached to the zipper pull. Skiing, hockey. Math. Knitting. This guy is an all-rounder.

"Yeah, I think Dad's there, too. We close at six on Mondays, so we'll head home for supper pretty soon."

"Nice."

"It is nice."

Our stuff is packed up now—his into a backpack, mine into a shoulder bag—and we make our way through the café and out onto the sidewalk, where we discover it has started to snow.

The flurry of snowflakes hits us in the best way, like when you're a little kid and snow is magic, so for a moment, we both stop there on the sidewalk, looking up at the wild effect of snow flowing around in the glow from the streetlights.

I hear him take a deep breath and I glance over. His eyes are closed and he's smiling. "This feels great, doesn't it?"

Actually, it feels pretty wintery, but I don't want him to think I'm a wuss, so I say, "Feels great after being inside for so long."

Across the street, in the window of String Theory, I can see Mom and Dad at the front desk. Talking. They're not looking our way, haven't noticed us yet. They're like actors in a show. They turn to each other for a moment, throw their heads back, and laugh. He puts his arm around her and hugs her. Yeah, my parents are pretty cute, although I wonder what Finn thinks.

I glance at him, and I see that he's looking at the scene in the window of String Theory, too.

"Do your parents ever fight?" he asks. "About work? The store? Working together?"

I did not see that coming.

And do they fight? No. Never. I shake my head.

"Nope. They call it 'discussing,' whenever they don't agree on something." *We're discussing it,* says Dad. *We're having a discussion.* Usually there's laughter. "Do yours? Fight, I mean?"

Considering that his mother is possibly cheating on her husband behind everyone's back, having secret conversations in the dark back hallway of String Theory, it wouldn't surprise me.

It takes him a while to answer, and I'm starting to feel sorry I asked, but finally he says, "Yeah. Yeah, they fight."

"I'm sorry." Not sure if this is the right thing to say, but the moment seems to call for something. He's not smiling. He's just gazing across the street at my parents in the window, who have now moved on to something else. I can see Mom, but Dad has disappeared. She's still talking, though, so he must be down the hallway.

The hallway.

Maybe this is the moment I should tell him. Tell him what I know about his mother. Would that help? Information like that?

"It's worse lately," he says.

Something about a few hours of communing over math problems, and all the other stuff, has obviously made him feel like telling me stuff. I've been around Anderson long enough to know that things can build up for a long time, and then you just have to let them out. Math contest prep and my parents across the street at String Theory and these swirling snowflakes have obviously pushed some button in Finn Nordin, and he's letting it out.

"I think something's wrong," he says. I'm not even sure he's talking to me anymore. "Something's going on with them, but I don't know what. Wish I knew, so I could help."

I think I know. Maybe this is the moment I should tell him. *Your mother is having an affair with a younger guy. Your mother is cheating on your dad. I heard her, over there in the dark hallway of String Theory.*

But I don't. And just as I decide it isn't a good idea, he turns to me and smiles.

"Sorry, don't mind me. Must be tired."

Why do I feel like I just backed away from a cliff?

"That's okay." I hope he can't hear the relief in my voice. I'm still a bit shaky about how close I came to telling him what I know. "We all think our parents are a bit, I don't know, weird."

We both look over at String Theory where my mother is living up to expectation by doing some dance behind the counter, holding giant skeins of baby blanket yarn in each hand, while my father accompanies her, playing percussion on the counter, using a pair of fat knitting needles as drumsticks.

Their timing is perfect. Finn laughs out loud, and, once I recover from my humiliation, so do I.

"Has anyone ever told you that you're easy to talk to?" he asks.

167

31. TELLING

I need to talk to you

> Sydney. Tuesday morning before school.

> *K*

Does she mean now? Phone? At school? In person? I wait.

I wait a long time. Long enough to finish breakfast, brush my teeth, braid my hair, make sure school stuff and laptop are stowed. Checking my phone the whole time.

Nothing more.

Which is worrying, because when someone says they need to talk to you, and then you don't hear another word, that means they really, really need to talk. Enough waiting.

You ok?

> *Meet you at the corner*

"The corner" is where our walking-to-school routes intersect. On walks home, it's where we debrief the day and shiver before heading off to String Theory (me) and Mrs. Bart's house (her). In the morning, we sometimes time it perfectly to arrive at the intersection. If Bethany is having a slow day, she sometimes meets us, too, but that's rare, since Bethany likes to get to school early and prowl the halls, checking out what's going on in the Central HS social scene.

K. On my way

Sydney is already standing at the corner. Long puffy coat with a red Canada scarf and mitts. Pack on her back and bump out front. Shifting around in place, probably to keep warm, and staring at the ground. She doesn't see me until I'm close enough to call out—"Here I am"—and she looks up, startled. She was a million miles away. Maybe somewhere in Norway.

"Hey, hi." She smiles, but it's not her real smile.

"What's up?"

She turns and starts walking. "I told him," she says.

Ah. I was right. Somewhere in Norway, where it's (quick time zone calculation) about two o'clock in the afternoon, Magnus Haugen is sitting in a classroom, or at his job, or hanging out with friends in a café, or throwing rocks down the ice at a curling club—all with the knowledge that he's about to become a father.

"What did he say?"

"He said I was lying. He said if I tell anyone, he'll deny it and

169

say I'm mentally unstable. That I'm a stalker. He said to stay away from him."

It comes out in a monotone rush. She's not crying, but her voice is not her voice. Tight, low, choked off.

"What?" I can't take it in. "How can he ...?"

"I thought about it and thought about it," she's spewing words now, and her voice is still tight and low as she walks. "I called my mom last night and she said I shouldn't do it, that 'there's nothing to be gained by telling him.' That it's not like we're going to get married and raise a baby. That it's better to just get on with it, get it over with, and get on with my life. He doesn't need to know. No one needs to know about him. She said the fewer people who know, the better. I told her—I told her to fuck off."

Okay, now there are tears. In her voice, on her face. She keeps walking, not looking at me. I glance around to make sure we're not going to run into anyone on the sidewalk anytime soon. There's a couple of Central students up ahead of us, but they're far enough away. A group on the other side of the street is so busy loudly dissecting last night's hockey game that I'm sure they don't even see us.

"I was so mad," Sydney is really struggling to get the words out now, as if her throat is closing up on her. "I hung up on her and emailed him right then. I told him there's a baby, that he's the father, that I don't expect anything from him, but he should know. And to let me know what he thinks, and let me know that he's—that he's okay."

I'm afraid to touch her because I learned a long time ago, with Anderson, that it's the kindness that kills you. When someone is just barely holding it together, that touch, that hug, that kind word is going to be the thing that tears apart whatever is holding them together.

So I don't touch her. I walk beside her and listen. "And what happened?"

She stops walking. Stops dead, surprising me so much that I have to turn around and walk a few steps back to her. She's staring off at some unknown spot in the distance (very likely in invisible Norway), mouth in a trembling straight line as she breathes and drips and the tears slide down her cheeks.

"He must have read it first thing in the morning over there, because his reply was waiting as soon as I checked this morning. He says I'm lying. He says the whole thing is a lie." She puts her hand on her bump, and for the first time looks at me. "I almost sent him a picture, but I thought that would be a bad idea. I mean, if he can be such an asshole about the truth, who knows what he'd do on social media with a picture of pregnant Sydney Bart."

We stand there looking at each other, and we both know she's right.

"He's an asshole," I say. "And you are amazing."

"I'm a pregnant idiot who just told her mother to fuck off," says Sydney, sniffling loudly. "Not so amazing." She shrugs.

I give her arm a pat then, and after a moment of half-grinning at each other about our different views of how amazing she is, we turn and start walking to school.

"Thanks," she says.

"You're welcome."

We walk a bit more. She pulls off a mitt and finds a tissue in her pocket and mops herself up, blows her nose.

"I know I'm going to get through this," she says finally. "I know my mom and I will make up. I know I'll be back on the ice with my team again and this will all be behind me one day. But right now, it's just so hard."

"I know."

We walk. I just stay quiet, waiting for her to work through her unhappiness, one stitch at a time.

"Life can be crap."

"Yes, life can be crap."

"So, what do you do?" she asks, looking at me. She's taller, so she's actually looking down at me. Her voice sounds more normal now and I can tell the crisis has passed. She just sounds kind of mad. At her mom, at Magnus Haugen. Maybe at herself, too. "When life gets so crappy?"

I smile at such an easy question. Up ahead I can see the

school, the hordes of students standing around in the chilly morning, not ready to start another day of classes and homework and structure and rules (which is actually all the stuff I love). I can see Anderson sauntering toward the front doors with Robert. I glance up at the second floor, wondering if Bethany is up there, looking out from the science lab and clocking who's talking to who, who's standing with who.

"Easy," I tell her. "When life is crap, I knit."

Because then I don't have to look too far ahead.

32. KNIT & NATTER AND WAY TOO MUCH INFORMATION

Wednesday night at String Theory, and Knit & Natter is going well. Mom is demonstrating how to do cables for a beginner hat pattern.

"So, look at these six stitches," she says. "These are the six stitches that you're going to turn. The ones that will make your cable."

I can just picture her standing up and going around the table to point out the six stitches on everyone's needle. They'll all be frowning at the stitches, frowning up at her, frowning back at the stitches. Because cables are like this magical transformation that seem undoable—until you do them. And then you can't believe how easy they are. A perfect example of The First Rule of Knitting.

"So now, just take the first three stitches off your needle, like this, and place them on your cable needle."

And then someone's phone rings. At least, I think it's a phone. The ringtone sounds more like a band at some swim-up bar at a Caribbean resort (not that I've ever been to a Caribbean resort, but I've seen movies. It looks like something I would never do. Ever.).

"I'm so sorry, everyone. I have to take this."

Lauren. The sound of a chair pushing back and the rustle of movement.

"No problem," says Mom, and then she's back to her lesson. "So, okay, have you got those stitches on your cable needle?"

Lauren scurries down the hallway.

Down the dark hallway and into the little alcove outside the washroom. And there I am, yet again, behind the curtain, curled up on the window seat. Needles still. Listening.

I would happily not listen, but it's difficult when the person whispering is almost close enough to touch. If she were to reach out and push the curtain aside, we'd be face to face. I hold my breath, hoping this does not happen.

"Hi, hi. No, it's fine. I'm at my knitting thing but it's fine." She's whisper-talking. The cable-makers can't hear her, but I sure can. "So, is it on?"

In the pause, I hear Mom: "Now you're going to work these three stitches on your needle, just work them like normal."

"Sure. Now? Where are you?"

Maybe it's Finn. Maybe he's calling from hockey practice. Or maybe it's Mr. Nordin, calling to say Ava needs picking up and he's at some meeting. Maybe I'm sitting here, silently eavesdropping on nothing more than normal Nordin family stuff.

"Is the wine chilling?" Whisper-giggle. "Sheets turned down? Hey ..." Her voice goes all—how to describe it—hot-romance, maybe. "Got your little packet?"

Not normal Nordin family stuff. Nope.

"No, I'm free for the evening. Knitting thing, then I said I was going to Elaine's. Dan's home with the kids, so I can be there any time."

I hold my breath, wishing this would end. I'm sitting here, listening to Finn's mother arranging a date with some guy. A date involving chilled wine, turned-down sheets, and a little packet. And I know what a "little packet" is, thanks to Mrs. Magid and our Health unit on intimacy, consent, and birth control.

"Okay," she says, after a short pause. "See you soon. Be ready. Bye."

Eew. I really, really wish I hadn't heard all that.

But I did.

Lauren, mother of Finn and Ava, is now drifting back down the hallway, back into the cable lesson.

"When you're twisting these stitches, they're going to feel tighter, and that's completely normal," Mom is saying.

"Oh, no, I dropped a stitch," Vela wails.

"I think I did, too." Oscar.

"I'm so sorry, everyone, but that was my husband." Lauren. "He's tied up and can't pick up Ava from dance. Again." I can picture her rolling her eyes as she lies to everyone, making it look good. *Oh, these husbands who can't live up to expectations, am I right?*

"Oh, that's too bad, Lauren. Sorry you missed my little demonstration here, but you can find a tutorial on our website, or anywhere on YouTube, really."

My mother is being all supportive, talking about knitting cables. She has no idea.

"Thanks, Rowan. Bye, everyone! See you next week."

The front door swishes open and closed. The curtains beside me flutter a little in the cold air and then go still.

"Bliss!" Mom calls down the hallway. "Can you come and help us with some dropped stitches?"

33. LUNCH OBSERVATIONS

Lunch hours have become a bit weird this week, now that James and Bethany appear to be sliding toward coupledom, and Sydney seems to be spending a lot of time in some distant world of her own, a world where Magnus Haugen didn't say those awful things and she didn't tell her mother to—well, where she and her mother are talking to each other. (They aren't.) She's been very quiet.

And then there's Anderson, who has become something of a celebrity at school since being named Athlete of the Month for October in the school board's varsity sports newsletter, thanks to Central's Senior Boys volleyball team riding a four-game winning streak. It all has something to do with Anderson's amazing skill at running "quick sets to the middle" or some technical thing that Coach Coslov is wowed by and other teams don't seem to be able to figure out. Apparently, all the guys who hit those big spikes over the net think he's a magician.

Yes, my friend Anderson has gone from being that big guy, in the triple-X T-shirt and shorts, to a star. His teammates high-five him walking down the hall. Some Grade 12s—could it be the "whale" guys from that first game?—nod hello as they go by our table. Bethany and I keep elbowing him, or each other. Is *this our friend Anderson? This celebrity?*

It is, but you'd never know it from Anderson. He just continues to stroll around, taking up a lot of space and being himself. Which means nice, friendly, quiet, smiling. I can tell he's in a happy place, which is not what either of us expected when we started talking about the possibility of him trying out for the team.

"What's up with you?" he asks on Thursday, the day after I heard far too much in the dark hallway at String Theory. Normally, we'd be in Mrs. Badali's room for 3C Club, but lunch clubs were cancelled this week because of some special faculty meetings.

"I don't know. Is something up with me?" I play it cool. Take a bite of my apple. Try to ignore the drop of mustard on his chin. Honestly, Anderson. Learn how to eat.

Also, I'm already wrestling with the pros and cons of telling Finn something. Maybe not the exact details, because, eew, that would be excruciating, but in light of our post-Beanbag conversation on the snowy street Monday night, maybe, just maybe, he should know about this?

And Anderson has obviously noticed that my mind is at work on a problem. Not a math problem, and not a knitting problem. He can tell that, yes, something is up with me. But he's willing to play along.

"I guess not," he says, smiles, lets his eyes slide past me to Taz Fenwick, who has tagged along with James today. Actually, he tagged along yesterday, too. And—wait a minute—also on Tuesday. And Monday, the day of our conversation at my locker. Oh, dear, he's been eating lunch with us—with me?—all week. He drifts in behind James, settles himself, usually next to me, and proceeds to smile and eat. And say very little. And smile some more.

Our conversations go something like this:

Taz: Hi, Bliss.

Me: Hi.

We eat and listen to the conversations going on around us. That's about it.

But today, Thursday, Anderson is digging. He thinks I'm acting weird because Taz is sitting here with us. Taz, my date for the Not Halloween Dance, a week away. Taz, who seems to have permanently joined our happy little club.

"Stop," I warn Anderson in a voice so quiet, only he can hear.

"Okay." He smiles, shrugs, takes another enormous bite of his ham and cheese sandwich, which produces more drips of mustard on his chin. Honestly, this guy.

My eyes drift to the far side of the cafeteria, where Finn is sitting with Karlee and Adele, and some other guys in our grade. They're talking about something interesting, clearly, because the whole group of them are leaning in, laughing, using their hands to accentuate points, laughing some more. Adele actually looks as if she's having fun. Adele, his cousin. *She's practically my twin*, he said. If I'm going to say something, maybe it could be at our next math contest prep, although, I'm not sure when that is.

"Hey, congrats on the Athlete of the Month thing," says someone behind me.

It's Cameron Tellez, following the Gang of Five toward the door, probably headed to the gym, where they often spend their lunch hours indulging their jockdom by shooting baskets. Peter leads, and the others follow, glancing back without much interest, but Cameron has stopped right behind my chair.

Anderson looks up (I'm happy to see the mustard is gone from his chin).

"Thanks."

Awkward moment as Cameron stands there and Anderson looks up at him with an expression on his face that can only be described as suspicious. It's a long moment. It ends when Peter yells from near the door, "Hey, Chippy!" (an unexplainable nickname from our elementary school days), and Cameron moves away without another word to join the Gang. I think he must have smiled as he left, because Anderson nods and smiles a bit, too. Like two normal people having a friendly interaction.

I'm looking at Anderson and, after a moment of watching Cameron walk away, he looks at me.

"What was that?" he asks, perplexed.

"That was Cameron Tellez being nice," I say, and I'm just gathering my words to tell him about that time in the gym, during the game, with Cameron and the "whale" guys, when I hear Taz say:

"So, Bliss, do you like cricket?"

And the moment passes.

34. THAT'S THE WAY TELLING WORKS

Sunday afternoon, again.

Auntie Bryn and I are curled up on the couch, again.

I'm knitting, again.

Mom just got home from the store and is in the kitchen throwing a veggie lasagna together. I did offer to take over, but she insisted we stay put.

"I need some kitchen therapy," she told us when she came through the door. "People were a little crazy this afternoon. Why? What is it about Sunday that makes it so hard to decide between alpaca and merino? Chunky or worsted? Knit or crochet?"

"Come and sit." Auntie Bryn nods at the big chair beside the couch. "Help me with this." She waves the Saturday paper in the air. Auntie Bryn is a cryptic crossword wiz who doesn't really need help, but she recognizes a sister in need.

"Tempting, but no, I'm going to go chop my frustrations

away." Mom gives my shoulder a squeeze on her way by. "Wielding a knife will help. Goodness." She leans over me and the sock I'm knitting at breakneck speed. "Your shoulders are tight. Loosen up, honey."

I'm knitting my brains out. Knitting a sock at record speed. I started the first one yesterday during my Help Desk shift and, because I had only one customer—Vela, whose cables were slipping sideways, thanks to her inability to count six stitches, but after much tinking, we got it fixed—I finished the sock in about three hours. I started the second one after lunch, and here I am, a few hours later, in the home stretch on its partner. Yes, my shoulders are tight.

But it's not the socks.

So, Mom's in the kitchen, chopping loudly and singing along to her oldies playlist. I think I recognize the Backstreet Boys ...

"Hey."

I don't look up from my needles. "Mmm?"

"What's up?"

I've been thinking about this, actually. About asking Auntie Bryn what she thinks I should do. I just didn't know how to start, but she's made it easy for me.

"What if," I say, but I keep knitting and don't look at her. "What if you knew something that could hurt someone. Would you tell them anyway?"

"Hurt someone. How?" Auntie Bryn lays the crossword down on her stomach, and I know she's looking at me, but I just keep my eyes on my needles. "Do you mean someone could be injured?"

"Not injured. Not injured physically, I mean."

She nods. "Okay, good." Pause. Maybe she's waiting for me to say more but I just go back to my knitting. "Is it Anderson?"

I shake my head.

"Okay." She waits.

I'm beginning to wish I hadn't started this.

"Are you going to tell me anything more? Or is this going to be a hypothetical case?"

I shrug. "Never mind."

"If it's on your mind, it's on my mind now, too, sweetie. That's the way telling works. I can't not mind." She frowns. "Wait, does that even make sense?"

Auntie Bryn trying to keep it light, and I love her for it, but it's not helping.

That's the way telling works. Like Sydney and Magnus Haugen. Telling him he was part of a baby-making situation sure didn't help either of them. In fact, it made everything worse. And telling me about it all didn't help, because I can't even do anything to help her, and I still have to carry the whole story around in my head. *Team vans, bonding, etc.*

So, what happens if I tell Finn that his mother is lying,

185

sneaking out of Knit & Natter to talk to her boyfriend on the phone and set up dates involving turned-down sheets? Is telling him going to help? Is he going to thank me? Who wants to hear that about their own mother? Maybe he'll hate me. I'm not sure I could stand that, so ...

"Nah, forget I said anything," I try to grin as if there's nothing chewing away at my insides. "It's hard being sixteen, you know." Diversion tactic: playing the teenager card.

She just watches me, waits a moment, then reaches out and squeezes my foot.

"It's hard being an old aunt, too. I'm here if you need me."

"I know." Knit, knit, knit. I don't know what I need right now.

"Okay," she says, peering at her crossword, pen poised. "*A month getting round an Irish county*. Four letters. Really, people? So easy. *Mayo*."

I just keep knitting.

35. LOCKER

"Hey, how's it going?"

I'm at my locker and have been taking quick glances to see if Taz is going to show up. He's done this a few times, materializing out of nowhere to stand there smiling and saying a few words like, "Hi!" and "Did you get your science homework done?" I think he's being coached by James, and maybe Bethany. Our longest conversation has been about cricket, and that was because I asked leading questions—"So, what does a typical game look like?"—so he had lots to work with. He has a slight English accent, which makes his voice pleasant to listen to when he gets going. This is a bonus, because most of the time he doesn't really have much of interest to say. (Okay, okay. That might be mean. But ... well, also true.)

But no, this morning, when I look around my locker door, it's not Taz Fenwick, but Finn Nordin smiling at me.

"Oh, hi!" I dive back into my locker, sure that every thought going through my head is written on my face. *Your mother is having an affair with some young guy. Maybe you should tell your dad. Maybe you should protect your sweet little sister.* I have to dig deep for a response. "It's going good. How are you?"

I'm struggling. He doesn't appear to notice, though.

"Great. Had a hockey tournament in Niagara Falls, so not much schoolwork done."

"Oh, cool." That's all I've got. I'm still down in my locker. A few minutes of silence as I continue to shuffle stuff around. This isn't going to work much longer.

"So," he says, after a too-long pause. "That email from Wenzik. After school today in the math room, right?"

Yes, an email about going over some problems together, seeing "where we're at," and making plans for the trip to University of Waterloo in a few weeks.

"Right." I pop back up and nod, while examining the pile of books on the shelf of my locker as if looking for something. I think he's waiting for me to say more, but I have no idea where to take this conversation so that it doesn't lead to his mother.

"No hockey practice today, and Ava's on some school trip, so this is a good afternoon for me," he says. A conversation starter for sure.

"Oh, good. It's good for me, too." I'm still staring at my books, still searching for something that isn't there. Escape, maybe?

"Okay then, see you in math class," he says, after a pause that goes on too long. I'm definitely failing in the social norms here. He starts to move away.

"Okay, see you." I throw him a farewell smile.

He's looking at me like he knows something's up. Like he knows that "you're easy to talk to" girl has disappeared and a "please go away I can't talk to you right now" girl has taken her place.

He gives a little wave, turns, and walks back down the hallway. Probably toward Karlee, and maybe Adele, waiting for him somewhere in the crowd.

Just for the tiniest of moments, I think about calling him back and telling him. Or at least doing something to erase the last few awkward minutes and starting a more normal conversation. But I don't. I slam my locker shut and walk in the other direction toward homeroom, convincing myself the whole way that I made the right decision.

36. CATS AND BLANKETS

"So today," says Charis, "we are going to work on a special and very easy project for the Humane Society."

Thursday, 3C Club in Mrs. Badali's classroom. She's at her computer, smiling and ignoring us as she tucks into some pungent stir-fry from the cafeteria. Also on her desk is a big mug that says KEEP CALM AND PRETEND THIS IS ON THE LESSON PLAN. Coffee, I think. She's taking frequent sips.

Everyone is here today—I was on attendance duty, and with the Clubs Showcase just before Christmas inching closer, those participation points for this session are becoming more valuable—so there's a full complement of twelve crafters waiting for Charis to tell us what this special project is. Sydney wasn't sure she could make it—something about a midwife appointment—but here she is, sitting at the back with Anderson and Amanda, not quite over the whole telling-Magnus and swearing-at-her-mother thing, but making an effort.

"Cat blankets," Charis says, and everyone laughs.

"*CAT* blankets?" Adele snorts. "I have a cat and he doesn't use a blanket."

"I have a cat," says Anderson, "and she crawls under blankets all the time."

I could hug him. Instead, I just throw him a grin and he grins back. Something tells me Anderson has Adele figured out.

"These are small square blankets. Or mats, really," Charis explains. "They use them in the bottom of their rescue-cat crates or cages. Nothing fancy. Just a little warmth to make the kitties comfortable while they wait for their forever homes."

"Awwwww," says Amanda, Anderson's little Grade 9 friend. "Poor little kittens."

"I agree, Mandy," says Sydney. "My grandmother has knit a dozen of these. Her cats love them."

That draws a look from Adele, who I think may be channelling her own cat right about now. Finn sees and throws a grin my way.

Yes, we're back on solid ground again. All I needed was a few days to let the *Tell Him* urge ease off, and it did. Our Monday afternoon session with Wenzik and math contest prep also helped restore order in my universe. It's hard not to feel back to normal when you're deep into solving a problem (*A long series of algebraic sequences leading to the big question: What is the value of x?*) with someone who enjoys diving in as much as I do. We came up for air when Wenzik said, "Wow. Clearly, we have a good chance of winning this thing. Especially if you two work together like that on the problems," and we all high-fived. The euphoria was somewhat squashed when we walked together to the front door of the school, still dissecting one of the more difficult problems, only to find Adele waiting there, killing time by listening to something on her headphones. She caught sight of us, pulled off her headphones, and said, "Come on, Finn. Supper at our house tonight."

And I thought to myself, just for a moment, *Why? Why at his cousin's house and not at home?* and then forcibly shut that down, returned his wave and smile. Off we went in opposite directions.

It was okay. Order restored.

"So, we have two easy patterns here," Charis continues. "And a ton of yarn, thanks to Bliss's parents at String Theory." A moment's break as she applauds in my direction and everyone joins in. "Everyone got your needles? Okay, come on up and select your yarn, and then Bliss and I will get you started."

Finn comes right over to where I'm helping to distribute yarn and says, "Oh, wow, Ava would love this."

"Would she? I'm sure she could manage the pattern," I say. "She picked that scarf pattern up so quickly."

"You've met Ava?" Adele is suddenly right there. "When?"

It sounds like a police interview, the way she says it, but Finn just laughs. "Oh, we're regulars at String Theory. Bliss is our guru. And Ava loved it," he says to me before digging into the yarn stash. He doesn't see the look she flashes me.

I just smile. Cranky Adele, I've decided, is someone who has not yet learned the first rule of knitting and spends way too much time looking ahead for danger.

"Here, you might like this one." I pull out a boring worsted in a dull grey colour with flecks of beige and she takes it with a "thanks," which tells me everything I need to know about Adele.

"We'll be donating some to the Humane Society," says Charis. "But of course, everything we make will be on display for sale at the Clubs Showcase in December, so make it good. Okay, here we go."

Needles, yarn, pattern. Cat blankets in progress.

"That girl does not like you," Anderson whispers to me, glancing over at Adele, Karlee, and Finn, in various stages of casting on. "I wonder why?"

I look up at him, because his voice and the look on his face say he knows exactly why Adele doesn't like me. I'm about to shoot that down, but we're interrupted.

"Oh, no, I did it again!" wails Amanda, and Anderson rides to the rescue.

37. NOT HALLOWEEN DANCE: PART ONE

It's not so bad, once I get there.

The getting there was a bit of an ordeal, though.

First, Mom comes home from the store while I'm getting ready. For me "getting ready" means having a shower, putting my hair up in a sort of topknot thing (because there's nothing worse than hair in your face while dancing, and I quickly apply the first rule of knitting to thoughts of dancing), applying two quick dashes of mascara and a swipe of lip gloss (Auntie Bryn is the make-up artist and she actually called to offer her services for tonight if I wanted them. I politely declined ...) and dressing up in my party clothes (a swirly, multicoloured tunic thing, picked up at One Of A Kind from the lady who had a booth near ours, black leggings, and my favourite black ankle boots). Going for artsy rather than too formal. Finishing touches include the antique dangling earrings Auntie Bryn gave me when I got my ears pierced and my grandmother's ruby ring, for good luck.

"You look gorgeous," Mom says when I come into the kitchen—to try to eat a grilled cheese sandwich while standing up at the kitchen island. Comfort food required tonight. Also, I'm too nervous to sit. Mom doesn't comment on this, thank goodness.

"Aw, Grandma's ring," she says, taking my hand. "It's good luck, you know. She always said it was a magic ring."

I smile and chew. I know the story—how Mom was wearing this ring the night she and Dad met at some university frosh-week icebreaker. No way I'm going to get into what kind of magic I hope does or doesn't happen tonight. The best magic would be for the whole thing to be suddenly cancelled so I can stay home.

But of course the only magic that happens is Bethany, with James and Taz in tow, actually arriving on time to pick me up.

The doorbell makes me jump and I scramble upstairs to brush my teeth and take a final look at myself in the mirror while Mom does front door duty.

I look okay, I guess. What does it matter, anyway? It's not like I care what Taz thinks. (In fact, I only have a vague idea of what Taz thinks about anything. Except cricket. He absolutely loves cricket and can talk about it for a whole lunch period.) This whole "Taz And Bliss Go To The Dance" was all Bethany and James.

I'm frowning at myself in the mirror. Great way to start an evening of normal teen social behaviour.

Truthfully, I'd rather be curled up in front of the TV, knitting.

"Bliss! What's taking you?" Bethany yells up the stairs.

I give myself a shake and manufacture a huge, awards-gala-red-carpet smile at the girl in the mirror. She smiles back, although she does not look convinced, in my opinion.

"Coming!"

"Have fun!" Mom finds the self-control not to hug me as we head out the door to the car. I catch her checking out Taz as I pull my coat on, and hope no one saw her give me the silent "Cute boy!" look.

He does look good, actually. The classic white shirt just showing at the collar of his sleek three-quarter-length dress coat is unexpectedly stylish. And his, "A pleasure to meet you, Mrs. Adair," with that hint of English accent, definitely made an impression on her. Yes, my mother is pretty easy to read.

But now we're way beyond magic and into reality.

"The bus'll be here at ten to pick up any passengers needing a lift," says Mr. Blake as he pulls up to the sidewalk down the block from Central to let us out. This was on instructions from Bethany, who insisted it would not be cool to be seen getting out of Daddy's car.

"Perfect, Dad. Thanks!"

"Thanks, Mr. Blake." James, Taz, and I slide out of the car and join the groups heading toward the door.

The music is already pounding. The air is full of it, and we can see through the glass doors to the hallway and the open gym doors, where the lighting is multicoloured and flashing in some party-mood light-show arrangement. Two teachers are stationed at the door as we join the line-up and receive what I suppose are the usual instructions (how would I know? This is my first school dance since leaving middle school): coats on the racks along this wall, lockers off limits, no wandering around the school unsupervised, absolutely no alcohol.

I process the details through a fight-or-flight fog until Bethany throws her arms around me, squeezes me tightly, and exclaims: "I'm so glad you're here!" and the two boys laugh at us.

"Come on," says Taz, and he takes my hand—which feels both weird and reassuring at the same time. "Let's dance."

38. NOT HALLOWEEN DANCE: PART TWO

It turns out Taz Fenwick is an excellent dancer.

Of course, much of what happens out there on the floor is the usual unassigned group flailing that I remember well from middle school. It was fun then and I'm relieved to discover it's still fun now. Bethany and James and Taz and I are quickly joined by Anderson and Sydney. We hop and sway and fling our arms around to the DJ's playlist. Everyone else seems to be doing the same. I get glimpses of The Gang of Five surrounded by a bunch of girls in our grade. And over there, Finn and Karlee. And Adele. And some of the basketball boys are part of their group ...

Lights flashing, music thumping, people cheering, laughing, yelling, hooting. It's loud and fun. And I have to admit to myself, it's okay. It's okay.

Taz moves very well. And of course, his perfect proportions (accented by skinny black jeans and blindingly white tapered shirt) help the overall effect. Lots of eyes on him, I can see. Lots of eyes on me, too, as people are clearly thinking something along the lines of, "Why her?" But it's all fine because I have a secret weapon: I know how to dance.

Yes, thanks to my dad, who grew up in a small farming town and spent many Saturday nights at the curling club or the community centre, dancing to live bands (lots of fiddle, he told me. Lots of rhythm guitar, and cheesy country songs sung by a man who owned the local feed store), I know how to dance. Two-step, waltz, a less Oktoberfest version of the polka. I can follow a lead and hold my own on the dance floor, thanks to my dad, who swung me around the kitchen to the songs on his Maxville Saturday Night Dance playlist. In middle school, Anderson and I were the stars of the show when Bethany would secretly ask the teacher in charge of music to put on the latest country hit.

So, when the music changes to a slow ballad, and there's that awkward moment as couples readjust so that they actually have to touch each other, Taz and I just slide into position, find the rhythm, and dance.

Okay, yes, I do find it a bit unsettling to be this close to him, but he moves so well and knows how to lead, so I just keep my eyes on the far wall, a few feet above everyone's head so I don't have to make eye contact with anyone, including him.

Which is good, because I can tell people are looking at us.

Mostly girls. Also, Anderson and Sydney, who might be the best dancers in the room and who keep swirling in close to us. Showing off? Or maybe checking on me ...

Taz and I don't talk, which is fine, because I've come to the conclusion that he doesn't really have a whole lot to say. He smiles into the air and hums along with the music. This works for me.

And then when the song ends and the crazy wild music comes on again, it's back to group flailing.

We take breaks, of course. At one point, Sydney drags me off the floor and over to the quiet side, near the "Bar," as everyone is calling it—a few tables of water jugs, juice, pop, and chips, supervised by teachers who are, basically, on yard duty.

"Well, he can move," she says, pouring herself a water and quickly downing it. "I think we've got the two best dancers in the room."

I just smile at her, glad that she seems back to her normal self after that Magnus Haugen episode. I wonder if she's made up with her mom yet, and I'm about to ask her, but I sense someone move in beside me. So I turn, and ...

"Hi, Bliss." Finn Nordin. He looks over at Sydney and raises his hand. "Hi, Sydney."

"Hi," she says, a huge, meaningful smile on her face as she looks at him, at me, at him, at me. "I'm going to go find Anderson. Bye, kids!"

So, Finn and I are now standing together near the refreshment table, and it's still pretty loud as the music has switched to something different. Bhangra.

"Oh, cool!" he says. "Look at Taz and James."

So far in this conversation, I seem to be channelling Taz, because I have nothing to say, but I dutifully look to where he's pointing and see Taz and James and a bunch of other boys, and some girls, too—rocking out their bhangra moves.

"Go, Taz!" people are yelling at him. Hooting. Swaying and holding their arms up, trying to dance along on the sidelines.

I see Anderson and Sydney trying some moves (not bad), and Peter Abela must have Punjabi roots because he has now been welcomed into the main group, and the Gang of Five are cheering him on.

I find myself laughing out loud and clapping, like everyone else—at the music, at the happy dancers, at the feeling of joy.

"This is brilliant!" Finn leans over and says into my ear.

"It is!" and when I turn to say it, our faces are inches apart.

Which freaks me out a bit—that little scar, his eyelashes, his mouth—but he doesn't notice because, even though he's leaning in to hear me, his eyes are still on the action out on the gym floor.

Thank goodness nobody saw.

The music wraps up and the gym explodes in cheering

and clapping. I see Taz, surrounded by people yelling their congratulations. Sydney is there. Bethany. Karlee.

Wait, Karlee? Yes, Karlee is holding on to his arm so he'll lean down and listen to her, and they're having an animated conversation, I guess about the dance. And then the music starts up again—not bhangra, some slow song—and Taz grabs Karlee's hand and whips her around, ballroom style, so that her arm lands on his shoulder, and his arm is around her waist, and they're dancing.

Yikes.

I'm about to glance at Finn to see if he's noticed but he gets there first.

"Oh, I love this song," he says into my ear. "Come on."

And now he has my hand and is leading me to the edge of the dance floor. It feels like slow motion but, suddenly, there we are, face to face, and his hand is on my back with just the right pressure to guide me, in step to the music. My left hand rests on his arm, then his shoulder (I can feel his muscles as he moves, feel his bones. How did my hand get there? Did I put it there? I can't remember). He holds my right hand—Grandma's ruby ring flashes at me once—and pulls it in, so our hands are joined, just filling the space between our shoulders.

"My mom and I used to dance to this one," he says.

"My dad and I used to dance around the kitchen. This song, and tons of others. The whole country music catalogue, mostly."

"Aren't we lucky. Parents who dance."

He looks down at me then and it's too much to take in because—well, I'm not sure why. Maybe thinking about his mother being so stupid and risking the happiness of this boy. *You awful mom. You're supposed to take care of your kids, not cheat on them.* A huge wave of fury rolls over me, followed by the strongest urge to tell him about it.

His hand squeezes mine, and I feel my grandmother's ring pressed into my finger for a moment. Magic? I wish I knew what he was thinking, right at this moment.

Okay, maybe not. This quiet place, here inside a noisy gym, is so much better than a dark hallway full of secrets. I bend my head into his shoulder and feel his chin rest just above my ear. I don't even hear the music anymore. I just hear him humming. The whole world is just this moment of us swaying side to side, and time stops.

Until the song ends, and it starts again.

We pull apart and look at each other with—maybe surprise?

"Wow, Bliss." His voice is not his normal voice. Yes, something just happened.

And just like that, I know I have to tell him.

"Listen," I say, moving in closer because the crazy music has started up again and I'm afraid he can't hear me. "I have to tell you something ..."

He leans over. "Sorry, what?"

"I have to tell you something," I'm practically yelling in his ear now. I need to drag him to a quiet corner and get this awful secret out in the open, where we can share it. *That's how telling works*. I'm sure it's the right thing to do now. We can figure it out together, but he needs to know.

"I have to tell you something," I try again, but before I can say more, we're interrupted.

"Karlee's looking for you," yells Adele over the music, grabbing his arm and ignoring me completely.

"Okay, just a minute," he says, and looks back at me, shaking his head. "What did you say?"

But the moment is gone. Especially with Adele standing there glaring at me.

"Nothing," I say. "It's okay."

He's confused, and I can tell he wants to say more—maybe even stay where he is. He glances at Adele and disentangles his arm from her grasp.

But it doesn't matter. No way I'm telling him now. Not with Adele standing there and—oh, look—here come Karlee and Taz, who are practically face to face and seem to have a million things to talk about, headed our way.

No. I just smile my best smile—I hope he doesn't notice that I still haven't resurfaced from that moment inside our dance—and wave him away. Smile the same weird smile at Taz, as Finn moves away with the girls, and tell him I think I'm going to have to call my dad to pick me up early. Headache. Not feeling great. Sorry.

"Do you want me to wait with you?" As he says it, he glances over his shoulder at Karlee, who is now hesitating at the edge of the dance floor and looking over at us. Finn has turned away, toward the dancers, all those flailing arms. Adele stands guard, as usual.

"No, it's fine," I tell him. "Go have fun. And thanks. It was fun." I have no idea what else to say.

"Yeah, it was fun," he says, and waves, but he's already moving away.

By the time I have my coat on and go out the door—phone out to call dad for a ride—Taz has already caught up to Karlee, Finn, and Adele.

Everything has changed. I'm not sure what happened, or even how. But as I stand there in the cold, just outside the glass doors, calling Dad ("I'm okay, really. Just a headache. Can you come get me?"), I feel the pattern unravelling, and I have no idea which stitch could possibly come next.

39. CAT FACES

Mom and Dad head off to String Theory without me on Saturday morning. I find a note on the kitchen table when I finally drag myself downstairs for breakfast after a night of lying awake, staring at the ceiling—followed by short periods of drifting off into a dreamland full of dancing, Taz's white shirt, my hand on Finn's shoulder—and then finding myself staring at the ceiling again. It's not very restful.

But I eventually fall into a deep sleep and don't even hear my parents leave, although I do have a feeling my bedroom door inched open at one point. One of them checking on me. *Is she breathing? Yes. Okay. We can go.*

The note: *Didn't want to wake you. See you later for Help Desk? If you're not up for it today, no worries. xo Mom and Dad*

Dad and I didn't talk much on the way home. "Headache," I explained. "Must have been the loud music."

"You need to get out more," Dad said, but I know he was kidding, and maybe even a bit worried about me, because he reached over and gave the back of my neck a gentle squeeze (which felt great, actually. A sort of instant massage. I had no idea I was so tense.).

He turned up the music a little, so that the voice of the female singer (Adele? Perfect choice) filled the space around us. I'm pretty sure he was letting me know there was no need to talk.

And I'm also pretty sure he knew there was more going on than a (real or convenient excuse) headache, and I know that he and Mom probably talked about me and this dance, and the whole Taz thing.

But I also know they will stay out of my way until I feel ready to talk about it. Which I in no way am. Ready to talk about it, I mean, because I'm still processing that it wasn't about Taz at all.

So, when I arrive at the store after lunch for the Help Desk, they just smile at me and carry on. Dad's at the cash, ringing up a pile of white and blue yarn for one of the NHL-logo blanket kits I did the graphs for (Maple Leafs, of course). It's a new customer who is loudly telling Dad she heard about this from a friend whose sister bought one, and won't it be just the best gift for her hockey-mad granddaughter? Mom is filling one of the shelves with a spectacular new hand-dyed rainbow-themed merino from Sue, the problematic supplier with the scary sheep.

I wave hello, go down the hallway, through the curtains, drop my coat on the window seat, and plug the kettle in. A cup of tea, my current project (a baby sweater with a self-patterning yarn that knits up magically in a gorgeous Fair Isle), and, hopefully, very few Help Desk clients. That's all I want today. As little interaction with people as possible.

Because I'm still processing last night and a pile of interactions that include multiple texts from Bethany, as well as a couple from Sydney and Anderson.

Bethany: *Why did you leave? Headache? Really? What happened? Why didn't you find me? Was it Taz and Karlee?*

Sydney: *Which dancer gave you the headache?*

Anderson: *You ok?*

And the interactions that happened even before that—dancing with Taz, which was pleasant and uneventful, sort of like the boy himself. And dancing with Finn.

Which was not uneventful, and something way more than pleasant. Inconvenient, because the boy has a girlfriend (as well as a guard dog cousin), and a mother whose secret bad behaviour is haunting me.

Just a headache, I text Bethany. *Better today. Help Desk!*

I decide not to get into it with Sydney because who knows where that would lead?

As for Anderson, just a quick *I'm ok. Thanks,* which he will definitely know means I'm probably not. But I'll deal with that later.

So, of course, when the door opens and Mom, now back at the counter with Dad, says, "Well, hi!" with such enthusiasm that I look up, I don't expect to see Finn and Ava Nordin standing there.

But there they are.

Several thoughts go through my head.

Why? (Quickly answered: Ava wants something from the Help Desk, of course. It has nothing at all to do with me and Finn—and that moment on the dance floor last night. Snap out of it.)

What happened with Karlee and Taz? (No answer for this one. Wait, Bethany would know something ... No. I'm not texting Bethany and getting into a conversation about this. The end.)

What do I say to him? (Which refers back to the first question.)

"Were you looking for Bliss?" Mom asks, once the front door greetings are done.

Silly question, Mom. They found me.

Ava has an excited smile on her face and is holding her knitting bag (a cloth book bag from the public library, which is perfect) and a notebook. She waves at me. "Hi, Bliss!"

Finn has a half-smile on his face and is holding nothing. Actually, his hands are stuffed in the pockets of his blue ski jacket. He does not wave, but he does say, "Hi."

"Hi." I decide the easiest thing to do is focus on Ava. "So, what have you got there?"

She comes bouncing over—yes, bouncing. Practically running. It's adorable.

"I've got this idea for cat blankets. Finn told me about the project you were doing at school and it sounded like such a good idea, and I was thinking about it and I did this. Do you think it will work? Could we do this? Finn says he thinks it will work but you're the expert, so we came to ask you. What do you think? See?"

She's talking quickly, dropping her knitting bag on the table and holding the notebook open. I glance up at Finn and he's just grinning at his sister because she's so cute in her excitement. And besides, no other words of explanation are required.

It's a graph-paper notebook, which stops me for a moment, because at Ava's age I had a notebook like this, too. Shading in boxes, filling them with letters and shapes and numbers, creating patterns. Hours of entertainment.

"See?"

She has to flip through the pages, but now she's found the one she wants and holds it up in front of me—so close to my face that I have to quickly lean back a bit in order to focus.

"Put it on the table, Avie, so Bliss can see." Finn reaches out and gently eases the notebook on to the table and the three of us lean in and look.

It's brilliant. She's created a stitch graph of a cat face. Ears, eyes, cheeks, nose, mouth. Okay, it's a little chunky, but still clearly a cat.

I stare at it in amazement, then look up at her. "You did this?"

Ava nods. "It was easy. See?" She unfolds a paper stuck between the next pages. "I just used this picture of a cat face, and then I matched the spaces and lines with the boxes on the graph paper. Finn showed me. He found a knitting thing that had a graph of a fox and I used that as an example and just did it. For the cat blankets. See? Don't you think the cats would like to have a blanket with a cat face on it?"

"I absolutely think the cats would love this," I tell her. "Mom, check this out."

My mother comes out from behind the counter and joins us at the table.

"Oh, my goodness, Ava, this is wonderful." She leans in for a closer look.

I glance at Finn, standing across the table from us. He's smiling at his sister. Proud of her, or maybe just enjoying how happy she is.

"Reminds me of another little girl I used to know," says Mom, pointing over at me. "Bliss used to do the exact same thing at your age, Ava." (Well, actually, I was younger, but okay.) "And now she creates patterns like these."

She points at the two blankets hanging on the wall over the shelf of worsteds and sport weight: one with a Blue Jays logo, and the other, Montreal Canadiens.

"Wow! You designed those?" Finn is impressed, gazing at them, then back at me.

Blush. Why am I blushing? I never blush.

"Yup." I'm articulate, too.

"Bliss, I think Ava is on to something, don't you agree?"

Ava beams at Mom, at me, at Finn. And of course, we all beam back at her.

"Okay, next step is to figure out how to fit the graph into the right number of stitches," I say. How to turn this rough series of shaded-in squares into a knitting pattern. My brain is starting to rev up and calculate, the way it does when I'm faced with a math problem ...

Which makes me think of the math contest. Which makes me think of Finn, still standing there.

When I look up, he's looking at me. Not smiling, exactly, just looking.

And then he looks away, at his sister: "Hey, Ava, remember I have to get over to Riley's for hockey, right? Mom said she'd be here," he glances at his phone, "in about ten minutes."

He looks at my mother. "Is it okay for Ava to stay here with you until my mom gets here? I mean, I can stay, if that's a problem. But I'll miss my ride to hockey, and ... well, I just wondered."

"Absolutely fine, Finn. Ava can sit here with Bliss and work on cat graphs and her knitting, no problem at all," Mom says. She smiles at him and turns to me. "Right, Bliss?"

"Absolutely fine." Yikes. I'm finally going to meet his mother. In person. I start counting squares in Ava's cat face graph to distract myself.

"Okay, great." He starts inching toward the door. "Okay, Ava? Stay here 'til Mom gets here, okay?"

"Okay." She doesn't look up. Her eyes are on my index finger, counting each square.

And with a "bye" all round, Finn is gone. For some reason, I feel the need to take a deep breath and steady myself. No one notices because right then, a customer comes out of one of the aisles with a skein of sock yarn and a whole list of questions for Mom, and the phone rings, which gets Dad occupied.

So now it's just Ava and me and our cat graph.

"This is fun," she says, and we smile at each other. Math-and-knitting girls at work.

It takes a bit of calculation, including rubbing out and reshading squares, before we get a pattern that we both agree on, but considering this was started by a nine-year-old, I'd say it's an impressive piece of graphic design, and I tell her so.

"Thanks," she says. And then, "What time is it?"

It's almost thirty minutes since Finn left, and there's no sign of their mother.

"It's almost two." That's odd. Ten minutes, Finn said. Ten minutes is a lot different from thirty minutes. "Have you got some knitting with you? Let's see how that scarf is going."

Distraction. She reaches for her library bag and pulls out her scarf, still on the needles but well along.

"It's going okay, I think."

"Okay? It's going great." That's no lie. Perfect, even tension, and no dropped stitches. A gorgeous soft, thick blue yarn. "That yarn is the perfect colour. It matches your eyes."

She shrugs. Ava is not up for compliments, I can tell. I can also tell that she has something on her mind, probably related to the fact that her mother did not arrive when Finn said she was going to. I'm really starting to dislike this woman.

"I hope my mom comes."

"Of course your mom's going to come and pick you up. Your brother said so, didn't he?"

She shrugs again. She has the needles in her hands, and she knits a few slow stitches—slide the needle into the loop, yarn around, slip it through and off, repeat—without speaking. Then:

"Mom was mad at Finn."

Oh, dear.

"That's too bad." Both of us, eyes on our stitches, one after the other. The next one. The next one. The store is buzzing with activity, but I feel as if there's a bubble around this little girl and me. Do I want to be here, listening to her tell me why their mother was mad at Finn? Is this a topic for the Help Desk?

Also, who could be mad at Finn? Come on.

"He told her how much I wanted to come here today, and that he had hockey, and she said she couldn't bring me because she had to be somewhere. And he asked where, because she always seems to be going somewhere. And Dad is away on some business trip this weekend and Mom was mad about that, too, so Finn said he'd bring me, but he couldn't stay, and she said, 'All right, all right, I'll retrieve her.'"

I'm knitting like mad, listening to every word and not daring to look at her. But she looks up at the end of this breathless account of life at the Nordin house, and I look over at her, trying not to show on my face what I'm feeling.

Because this does not sound good.

Do your parents fight? He asked me this question that night, out on the snowy street as we watched my parents being silly with drumstick knitting needles and big skeins of baby blanket yarn.

"Parents, eh?" I smile at her. Try to make it better for her, but she doesn't smile back.

"I hate it when my mom talks to Finn like that."

"I'm sure." We've both stopped knitting. "He's a nice big brother, is he?"

Sure, let's talk about Finn, instead.

"He's the best big brother," she smiles. "He's so nice. Much nicer than my friend Sara's brother. He's mean."

"Oh, dear. Poor Sara!"

"He hides her things, like her skates, and her favourite stuffy from when she was little. Don't you think that's really mean?" She's outraged, which is good.

"I do. That is so mean."

We return to knitting, and I hope that's it for the family secret reveals, but nope, there's more.

"Why were you and Finn acting so weird just now?"

Yikes. I keep knitting.

"Were we acting weird?" *Were we?*

"Well, he was. All quiet and just standing there," she says. "Like he was thinking about something."

Ava reminds me so much of me, it isn't even funny. The questions, the observations, the worry. This could be me at that age (well, at this age, too).

"Maybe he was just overwhelmed by your fantastic graphing skills." I try to keep it light.

She's not buying it.

"Nope. He was thinking about something." She shakes her

head. "Maybe he's still mad at Mom. Or maybe he didn't have fun at that dance thing he went to last night. Did you go? Did you see him there?"

Okay, we're getting on to dangerous territory here and I need to think of a roadblock, quick ...

But I'm saved by the arrival of the missing mother.

"So sorry, Rowan!" She breezes through the door in her red coat and tartan scarf, tossing her hair back as she peels off her sunglasses and looks around.

"No problem, Lauren. See? Ava's having a great time with Bliss."

"Hi, Mommy." Ava smiles at her mother and returns to knitting.

"Hello, my darling. How are you doing? Oh, that's gorgeous." Lauren, up close, is beautiful. She could be a model. No wonder her kids are so great-looking. She leans over Ava and drifts a finger over the scarf, which really is impressive.

And then she raises her eyes to me.

"And you must be Bliss. Hi. I've heard so much about you." She smiles, friendly and warm, just like somebody's mother meeting her kids' friend for the first time. "Math contest and knitting clubs. You are busy."

"And Help Desk," says Mom. "And she's usually around for Knit & Natter, too."

Oh-oh.

Lauren turns, eyes on me like two headlights. "I don't think I've seen you there."

No, Mom. No.

"Oh, Bliss usually hides out with her knitting in the back room during our sessions," Mom says, totally unaware of the damage she's about to wreak. "She just listens in from the window seat and jumps in to help when we need her, don't you, Bliss?"

A pause, then Lauren says, "Oh, lovely." But I can hear it, even if Mom can't: Lauren putting two and two together. *Back room. Window seat. Hides out. Listens in.* She stands up straight and adjusts her scarf, and she says to Ava, "Come on, honey. Time to go."

"All right." Ava carefully wraps up her yarn and needles and stuffs them into her bag. She lifts her coat from the back of her chair and shrugs into it, looking at me. "So maybe we can do a cat blanket? With a cat face on it?"

"I'll do one for practice to see how it goes, and then if you want, we could do one together." I never take my eyes off her face because I'm determined not to look into her mother's eyes. "Maybe your mom or brother could bring you next week."

"Well, we'll see," says the mom. "Thank you."

She's standing there beside Ava, and I just know she's staring at me, so I finally look up.

Yup. She knows. She knows I heard her. She knows that I know.

"You're welcome," I say, looking right at her.

She blinks and looks away first.

40. ROMCOM IN REAL LIFE

Sunday morning is spent managing communications from Bethany. She wanted to come over on Saturday for a debrief, but I pleaded recovery from headache and Help Desk as excuses. And she was going to be busy on Saturday night, because ...

Bethany, it turns out, is in love: James is The One. She texts me on Sunday morning as I'm lounging in my room, trying to decide between math contest prep and cat blanket knitting.

I've never ever felt like this about anyone!!!!!

I send her lots of smiley emojis and hearts and let her carry on without drawing her attention to the long line of boys she has crushed on, danced with, declared undying love for and, eventually, dumped (or been dumped by). Bethany is a romcom come to life. Poor James.

She does take a moment to look away from the mirror briefly.

You and Taz. Taz and Karlee. You and Finn??? That was weird

Was it weird? Surprising, maybe, since Karlee and Finn are a couple. But, hey, it was just a dance, right?

No big deal

Maybe she'll drop it if I play it cool.

Nope. My phone rings. I can hardly say hello before she's into it.

"So, did you break up with Taz, or what?"

Break up with?

"Um, I didn't know we were a couple."

"Well, you go to a dance together. And you dance like that together ..."

"Like what?" I don't get it.

"You know, all Dancing With The Stars moves, like real dancing."

Is that what Taz and I were doing? It just felt like the kind of thing Dad and I have done forever around the kitchen, and it was nice that Taz actually knew how to do it, too. I'm not sure Bethany, with her reality-TV-show filter, can understand.

"He's a good dancer," I say, trying to add a shrug to my words. "He's just kind of, I don't know, boring."

A silence. I picture her staring across her room with her mouth open. For Bethany, it's just possible that perfect proportions are more important than being able to keep up intelligent conversation.

"Oh." Pause. "So, when he and Karlee got together, that didn't bother you? I thought maybe that was the, you know, head-ache thing."

"Well, I was dancing with Finn, so we kind of made a perfect square, when you think about it."

"Stop making this about math," she says. "And yes, you dancing with Finn. What about that?"

Enough. I don't even know what to say about dancing with Finn, except that it was—well, it was certainly something. And in her current love-is-in-the-air mood, that wouldn't be a good idea.

"Nothing about that. Nice dance with a nice guy. Then home because I really did have a headache." *Liar, liar, pants on fire.* "But I'm glad you guys had fun. And, hey, what about Anderson and Sydney on the dance floor? And that awesome bhangra session!"

That keeps her going until we circle back to her and James, which is fine. I switch to earbuds and grab my knitting—the cat blanket based on the graph Ava and I designed. But I don't tell her about that, either. I just let her talk.

41. BEHIND THE CURTAINS

I don't always go into String Theory on Sunday afternoons, but today it seems like a good idea.

Auntie Bryn will be over later, and I don't think I want a one-on-one with her today. Too muddled in my own head. Too many questions I haven't even answered myself. I don't need her sharp eyes seeing everything I'm not saying. She has a gift for that. And I know the first thing she'll ask about is the dance, so, no. Time to run and hide.

Sydney texted on Saturday: *I want to marry Anderson. He is the nicest guy I ever met.*

I texted back: *Get in line*

We went back and forth on dance follow-up, but unlike Bethany, she doesn't dig in about the Taz-Karlee-Finn-me dance situation. *It was fun, the music was great, how about that bhangra stuff, Anderson is an awesome dancer, slept most of Saturday, not used to partying anymore.* That kind of thing. She was planning to spend Sunday sleeping, doing homework, and watching curling on TV with her grandmother. Did I want to come over?

No thanks. Have fun. Knit a cat blanket.

Sitting in Mrs. Bart's family room watching curling sounds cozy and all, but I'm not sure that's the answer to my jittery brain right now.

But I know what is.

So here I am, curled up on the window seat at String Theory, down the hallway, behind the curtains, hidden from all the Sunday afternoon activity happening out in the store.

And it's happening out there. Clearly, most yarniacs are not home watching curling this afternoon. No, they're here in our little shop, buying supplies for those projects that crafters need to make Christmas presents and wile away the winter. Mom and Dad are busy. Happy, but busy. Nobody bothers me. No Help Desk. No requests for another pair of hands. I think they know I just want to hide out for a while in my cozy corner.

I don't even realize that Anderson has arrived until a large hand pulls one of the curtains aside and there he is.

I was so deep in thought—and not about the next colour change on the cat blanket graph, either—that he startles me.

"Found you," he grins, coming in and pulling the curtains closed behind him.

"I wasn't hiding."

"I know."

He stands there taking up a lot of space and just looking at me. "So?"

Oh, Anderson. We haven't texted since that one short exchange on Friday night, but he knows me so well. I let out a shaky sigh as he unzips his jacket and throws it under the counter that holds the kettle and microwave and our tea things. He leans there, watching me.

"Come on. Tell me," he says.

"There's nothing to tell you." I shrug. Which is a big lie, of course, because there are a million things I could tell him.

What it felt like to dance with Finn, who has a girlfriend and a mean cousin and a sweet little sister, and a mother who is cheating on her family with a young guy. A mother who now knows I'm the enemy.

And the crappy secret that Sydney shared with me that she now has to carry around, reminded every day by the expanding bump in her body that there's a jerk on the other side of the ocean who thinks she isn't worth his attention, or care, now that the deed is done.

And does Anderson know that Cameron Tellez likes him? Because that's what I think, now that I look back at a few unexpected interactions over the past few weeks. How do I even go there?

"Right," he says.

"I just have a lot of things to think about right now, that's all."

I keep my eyes on my knitting. This funny cat face, designed by a little girl, who noticed that her mother was mad, and that her brother was sad and acting weird with me.

Her brother. Yes, for someone who has always found boys a bit of a puzzle not worth solving, I seem to be spending a lot of time thinking about this boy.

"Do you think maybe you think too much?"

"Come on, Anderson. How is that even possible?"

"It's possible, Bliss," he sighs. "And you do it. A lot. To you, everything is a problem to be solved. Or a pattern to be followed." He nods at my knitting.

I look down at the cat face, and picture Ava and her excitement yesterday, before her mother arrived and ruined it all.

"Remember the geese?" he asks me.

Grade 4. Mr. Oliver tells everyone to look at this picture of geese flying in a V. One line of geese is longer than the other, and he asks us to think about why that might be.

I put up my hand.

"Yes, Bliss?"

"One line is longer than the other because it has more geese," I say, pointing to the screen. "Fourteen on one side, ten on the other."

Fourteen is higher than ten. More geese. Longer line. Makes perfect sense.

Mr. Oliver squints at the screen, and I'm pretty sure he's actually counting the birds in the photo. Then he turns back to the class, to me, and grins.

"Well, okay, but no, Bliss," he says. "That's not it. Not the answer I'm looking for."

I frown. I'm right and I know it. Fourteen geese in one line, and ten in the other. That makes one line longer. It's so simple. Staring him in the face, but he can't see it.

He then goes on to explain about geese not flying straight into the wind, but across it, and the one line of birds is blocking the wind for the other line, so the protected side is longer, which means more birds.

He turns back to me and smiles.

"See what I mean, Bliss?"

Everyone's looking at me now, and it's uncomfortable to feel all these eyes on me, so I just nod.

But ...

I understand about wind and resistance and physics, but I know I'm right. One line is longer than the other because it has more birds in it.

Sometimes the answer is simpler than you think. Sometimes it's right there in front of you. Is Anderson right? Do I think too much about solving problems, looking ahead, getting it all right?

The fact that I am even asking myself this question is probably all the answer I need. Why do I suddenly feel cold and hot at the same time? Why can't I knit the next stitch? Why is a tear oozing out of my eye and sliding down my cheek ...?

I want to move, I want to wipe that tear away, but I can't. I'm frozen.

Anderson has been leaning on the counter, but now he comes and eases me over with his bulk so that we're squished together on the little window seat. He reaches one arm around my shoulders, solid and comforting.

"Stop thinking so much, Bliss. Just feel."

But I don't want to feel. It's so much easier just to look at the problem and solve it. Follow the pattern and knit it. Trust the process and find a way through to the end.

Don't look too far ahead.

"I feel, Anderson. Don't think I don't feel things," I whisper.

"I know." He squeezes my shoulders.

"Ouch." I don't think Anderson realizes just how strong he is.

Or maybe he does.

"Exactly, Bliss. Whether you keep them in or share them, feelings can hurt."

We sit like that for a long time, while the voices out in the store babble and shift, up aisles and down. Dad laughing at something, Mom answering a question about circular knitting. The door opening and closing. String Theory on a Sunday afternoon.

"I have to tell you something," I say finally. "Something about Cameron Tellez."

42. IN LIKE A LAMB

Sydney has started missing a few days of school every week. It's now November, and the bump is getting larger as her due date approaches, she says, sometime in early December. She's hoping it will be sooner, and I can completely understand. Even as tall and strong as she is, that is a lot of extra stuff to carry around. And not just the stuff attached to her body, either.

"I'm okay," she says at the corner on this unusually mild November morning. There's enough warmth in the sun to make you believe that winter has passed by and it's actually spring already. *March and sometimes November come in like a lamb,* Auntie Bryn said as we sat around after supper last night playing Scrabble at the kitchen table. *You know what that means.*

Well, the lion that's supposed to lead March out, and possibly this November, is still a few weeks away, and I've got a lot to think about before then. Right now, it's Sydney, walking beside me with a sort of side-to-side rhythm. No, not a waddle.

"When I start waddling, call the ambulance," she told me last week.

She's trying to be all light and in charge of the situation, but I see the set of her mouth. That's not a relaxed *all-good* smile; that's an *I'm-not-enjoying-this* fake smile.

"You okay?" I ask as we walk along the sidewalk at a suitable pace for a pregnant sixteen-year-old.

"I'm great," she says.

And that's all I can ever get out of her. Our conversation about Magnus Haugen has been filed. Sometimes she tells me tidbits from her midwife appointments ("They're big on breathing." "My glucose is perfect."), but not much. Which is just fine with me. She also told me that she and her mom are speaking again, which filled me with relief. I wonder if Mrs. Bart was part of that process, being the good manager of people that she is. After all, I wouldn't be here walking down the sidewalk with Sydney, if not for her.

"How are you?" she asks, and I'm drawn back from my images of Mrs. Bart wagging her finger at Sydney and her mother, telling them to smarten up.

"What? I'm fine."

"Ready for the contest?"

Loaded question, and she knows it.

Since the dance, Finn and I have been keeping our distance. Sure, we still have our practice sessions with Wenzik after school once or twice a week, if Finn's available. And sure, those are productive and fun.

Like when we're working on a question: *If the smaller triangle has sides of 3, 7, and 5, what is the perimeter of the larger triangle?* and Finn suddenly asks me:

"Why was the obtuse triangle always upset?"

"Um, because ...?"

"'Cause it's never right."

We both laugh, look at each other laughing, and turn back to math questions.

But no more extra practices over hot beverages at The Beanbag. And it's been weeks since he brought Ava to see me at the Help Desk, which is too bad, because her cat face blanket design has been a huge hit at 3C Club.

Ah, yes, 3C Club. Since the dance, there's been no sign of Finn, Karlee, or Adele at our weekly sessions. The other group members have really stepped up, though, and we've churned out a pile of cat and puppy blankets for the Humane Society, and some small comfort blankets for the women's shelter.

But no Finn and his entourage. They're going to come up seriously short on those participation points this session unless something changes.

That's not my problem, however. My problem is that I notice him. I notice him when he's there at math contest prep, or in the classroom, or walking down the hall with his friends. I notice that he and Karlee and Adele eat lunch together, but is it my imagination, or are they not hanging out together as much as before? I notice that he's different, for some reason. And this is a problem, because all I can think about is his stupid mother and her bad choices. And, yes, that dance.

"I'm always ready for a good math contest," I say. Keeping it light. *Bliss, the math girl.*

Sydney doesn't pursue it. Maybe she's too focused on her own discomfort to see beyond her bump (which is completely fair), or maybe she doesn't want to be like Bethany, who keeps pointing out that Taz has now joined Finn, Karlee, Adele, and their gang at lunch in the cafeteria.

"Nice guy," Bethany complains. "Dumps you, just like that."

"How's James?" I ask. It's so easy to change the subject with Bethany these days.

So, on a sunny, mild November morning, my pregnant friend and I are walking slowly toward another school day.

"Wonder if Wenzik's going to go over that quiz from last week," she says.

"Probably. Did you finish your English essay?"

"No. Tonight. Did you?"

"Yeah."

Sydney and I walk and talk, but not about anything that really matters to either of us.

43. POST-GAME

Anderson's volleyball season comes to a close with one spectacularly exciting loss on Thursday afternoon.

It comes against Westview, the school from the other side of the expressway. The "tough" school, everyone calls it, but I don't know why. They all just look the same as our guys out there on the floor. Tall, muscular, a bit scary in their fist-bumping and rah-rah-ing after winning points. Typical boys, as far as I can see, and not all that different from Central's players.

Well, except for Anderson, of course. Anderson stands out anywhere he goes, although I don't even notice his size anymore. He's always been the big bear to my little—what am I? A deer maybe? A bunny? Small, timid, looking for a place to hide away behind a math problem or a pile of yarn. Or a very large childhood friend. We make the perfect team.

"Way to go, Varga!" I think Sydney might be his second

biggest fan, next to me. Even Bethany, who loves him as much as I do, doesn't yell that loud. Sydney draws a lot of attention wherever she goes—I mean, being a pregnant Grade 11 student will do that—but everybody loves her yelling. I wonder if her ability to yell like that comes from her curling experience ...?

The unhappy Central players are coming off the court now, and I can see Mr. Coslov doing some serious talking to Anderson, who has to lean down a little so he can hear his coach. Head nods, shoulder pats. Smiles. Looks to me like Anderson just made next year's team.

Sydney is getting a lift home from her grandmother, and Bethany is off with James to do homework together, or something, so I wait alone for Anderson in the hallway. He comes out of the changeroom, floppy hair still wet, lugging his gym bag, and looking as if it's just another afternoon at the end of practice.

He sees me and grins.

"Aww. My fan."

"Always." I hug him. Hugging Anderson is like being enveloped in a giant sleeping bag. It's the best. "Are you sad?"

"Nah," he says as we turn and start walking down the hallway toward the exit doors and the cold walk home in the November chill. "It was a good season. And they played great."

"I'm guessing Coslov wants you back next year?"

"That's what he says." He shakes his head and grins at me. "Too bad I wasted a couple of years on the sidelines."

"Well, you're a star now, so that's something to look forward to, right?"

We're almost at the doors when someone calls out—"Hey, Varga!"—and we both turn.

And there is Cameron Tellez jogging down the hall toward us.

I did not see that coming. Well, okay, maybe I did.

Since telling Anderson about (a) Cameron and the "whale" boys in the bleachers, and (b) the possible significance of Cameron stopping by our table to congratulate him on the varsity prize, things have—happened.

Things like, Anderson and Cameron being seen walking down the hallway together with no other members of The Gang of Five in sight. Things like, Cameron sitting with us at lunch, an event that actually shut Bethany up for more than five minutes. (It didn't last, because they started talking about a new Netflix series involving a super-cool undercover revenge artist with a fabulous wardrobe and she once again found her voice.) Things like, Anderson saying to me, "Don't ask. We're figuring it out." Which made me smile.

Telling worked okay this time. At least, so far.

So Anderson and I, and Cameron Tellez are walking away from school in the cold, November twilight, talking about the volleyball game, and homework, and a shared love of vinyl ("My parents have an amazing collection of Studio Ghibli soundtracks, all on vinyl," Cameron says, which makes me stare at him with envy), and that's when he says, "Hey, I'm going over to Northfield Mall tomorrow night for the big pre-Christmas sale at Crateland. Do you guys want to come?"

Crateland—the best store for vinyl records in the region. Named (by Steve, the long-haired hippie who runs the place) after the tacky plastic grocery crates he uses in his displays. According to my parents, this is how everyone stored their vinyl records at university.

"Road trip," says Anderson, smiling at Cameron. "I'm in." He raises his eyebrows at me. "You in, Bliss?"

I just look at him for a moment, mouth open. Awkward. Is this a date? Am I going to be an inconvenient third in what I suspect is a budding relationship between these two guys, one of whom I love, and the other—well, I don't quite know what to think of Cameron. I've known him since kindergarten and he's never really impressed me in any way. Although this whole conversation has been promising.

"Come on, Bliss," Cameron says. "My sister and her boyfriend are going, too, so we can hitch a ride with them."

Anderson nudges me. Maybe he wants me along, like a favourite stuffy?

"Sure, okay."

"Great," says Cameron, just as we arrive at his corner. "I'll text you," he says to Anderson, who nods. "Great season. Don't be too sad."

Anderson laughs. "No. Not sad."

"See you later. Bye, Bliss."

"Bye." We wave him off and then turn and start walking again.

Nothing for about a minute, then Anderson bumps me with his arm and says, "Shut up."

I just smile, walk, smile, glance at him.

He's smiling, too.

44. MALL

Northfield Mall is super busy on a Friday night, so tagging along with Anderson is helpful. He takes up space and he tends to clear it as well.

He doesn't notice this gift of his, of course.

He and Cameron and I are strolling along—I tend to hang back a bit, let them act like my personal icebreaker, or maybe a cowcatcher on a train—checking out some of the vendors set up in the mall concourse. (Oh, no, is that the crazy sheep lady? Sue? It is! Duck behind Anderson, quick.) It's some kind of pre-Christmas craft sale, apparently. The boys just stopped at a woodworker who has a gorgeously crafted Settlers of Catan board on display. Out of our price range, which is too bad, because I can tell Anderson loves it.

We haven't even made it to Crateland yet, with all this other stuff to see.

Cameron's sister, Sofia, thinks our adoration of vinyl is "environmentally unsustainable" and that we should download (after purchasing, of course) all our music to our devices.

"What are you going to do with all those albums, Cam? What about when you go to university? Or move into an apartment? Mom and Dad's collection is bad enough."

She's talking to us over her shoulder from the front passenger seat while her boyfriend, Ben, drives. Ben is the quiet type. He probably has to be because she talks a lot. They're both Environmental Studies majors at the local university. I remember her from elementary school, a few years ahead of us, being involved in everything. Science Club. Choir. Safety patrol. I have a feeling Cameron might have one of those siblings who's hard to live up to.

It doesn't appear to bother him, though. He just shrugs. I know he shrugs, because the three of us are squished together in the back seat of this little car of Ben's, and Anderson takes up a lot of space. I'm in the middle, sandwiched between them. Any movement by my companions makes its way to me.

"Hasn't been a problem for Mom and Dad," Cameron says. "I'm not worried." And he leans a bit forward to catch Anderson's attention. "Hey, did you hear about the new release from Kids' Club?" and they're off on a vinyl wish list conversation. I could join in, but I don't. I'm enjoying listening to them. Also, it's kind of fun to watch Cameron Tellez in action, as a nice guy squished next to me in a car, rather than as a marauding member of The Gang of Five.

You just never know about people, do you?

So here we are, strolling together at the mall, and the boys are now checking out some gaming-themed metal art, but I take one look and know it's not for me. There's Sue and her deliciously well-stocked yarn display up ahead, so, yes, why not go say "hi"? I can report back to Mom, and Sue will probably tell her she saw me, and it will be good for String Theory public relations.

But just as I step out around Anderson's bulk to walk ahead, and just as I glance over to make sure there's a path through the crowd, I see them.

They're sitting close together at a little table set up around the side of Coffee Central, away from the throngs of shoppers and the buzz of activity. A little haven of calm. Private, out of the way.

Lauren and some guy. Some *young* guy.

I keep walking, turn my face away, hope she doesn't see me.

But I see her. With her red coat tossed on the back of her chair, her tartan scarf draped over the shoulders of a loose-fitting, white cashmere (I'm sure it's cashmere) turtleneck, a coffee in her hand. Leaning toward each other talking, eyes on each other. Her hair falling loosely so her face is partly hidden.

But not enough to hide the curve of her mouth as she smiles at this guy. Yes, a young guy. He doesn't look much older than Ben or Sofia. Longish black hair. Leather jacket and jeans.

Amazing how much detail you can absorb when you're hurrying by, trying not to see or be seen. A lot of detail. Most of which I wish I hadn't absorbed.

Because I'm no expert, but that is most definitely a couple sitting there gazing into each other's eyes.

And one of them is Finn's and Ava's mother.

"Well, hi, Bliss," says Sue, a bit too loudly, as I suddenly find myself in front of her display. "Nice to see you here. Your mom with you?"

"Hi." I glance over my shoulder and back. Are we far enough along, out of the line of sight? Is it possible Lauren saw me? My quick glance shows me that she's still looking at the guy. Good. This is good. I smile at Sue and her over-the-shoulder braid, which seems to be longer than I remember, and her handknit vest in a combination of pastels and neutrals, which just doesn't work, in my opinion. *Stop thinking, Bliss.* I reach for a skein. "No, I'm here with some friends. Wow, I love this angora. So hazy and soft."

And we talk yarn. I can talk yarn in my sleep, so this is good, because I'm not sure I'm capable of forming intelligent sentences at the moment. Sue has no problem filling any conversational void. ("It's the drugs," I can hear my father's voice. I think he's kidding about this, though.) After a few minutes, Anderson and Cameron show up beside me.

"You have beautiful wool," Anderson says to her.

"Why, thank you." Sue is momentarily stalled by his size, but not for long. "Are you a knitter, like Bliss?"

We go off on a brief Crafting for Community Care Club explanation, and when Sue asks Cameron if he knits, too, he says no, but he'd like to learn, and I have to bite my lip so I don't squeal at the pain Anderson causes as he carefully presses on my foot to make sure I don't comment on this.

We get away soon after.

The boys are chatty and laughing, but I just feel dazed. Too much to process. So it's good when we finally get down the long mall corridor to Crateland and split up to explore our musical passions. (I'm all about Classical right now; Anderson has a few bands he follows, as well as classic rock, and Cameron is trailing him. Good.) The store is busy. Steve, the famous proprietor (he was a roadie for one of those 90s country-rock bands and has stories, apparently) chats loudly with anyone who comes to the checkout to ask a question.

It's a good place to hide, so I do, trying to keep thoughts on LPs, and Steve's laugh, and not on the thought of why someone who's cheating on their husband would be out in public at a mall, one town over, where anyone could walk by. Surely that's using terrible judgement. But then, cheating on your husband—and your kids—isn't exactly using good judgement, is it?

But the fun isn't over because, just as I'm staring blankly at the back of a Deutsche Grammophon recording of the Third and Fourth Brandenburg Concertos with Herbert von Karajan, and look up (because Steve is laughing loudly with someone at the counter), I see a familiar face in the stream of people passing outside the store.

Adele, looking cranky as she trails along with some woman who looks equally cranky. Her mother?

She doesn't see me. They're headed in the opposite direction from that little coffee shop, with its special couple tucked away at that table around the side. In fact, they probably walked by it just a few minutes ago. But now, as I watch, they seem to be walking toward one of the exits. Cranky and tired. Not talking excitedly about seeing someone they're related to ... behaving badly.

"Hey." Anderson is suddenly beside me. "We're hungry. Want to go to the food court?"

"Sure!" I most definitely do. It's on the second floor of the mall, away from all the vendor displays and the crush of shoppers. I slide Herbert and J.S. back into place. "Let's go." Fries. Smoothy. Ice cream ...

Steve waves at us as we leave—Cameron bought three LPs, which I'm sure is going to cause some heated conversation with Sofia on the drive home—and we head out into the mall and up the escalator. The boys talk about Cameron's musical tastes, and I just listen and nod and smile. I'm having trouble finding words right now.

There's a perfect view of the coffee shop from the escalator, and if I wanted to, I could look back as we go up, up, up. But I don't.

45. TOLD

Help Desk. Saturday afternoon.

String Theory has seen a steady flow of shoppers today, but it's been quiet here at my table, so I've taken the opportunity to block out last night's revelations (Finn's mother is truly acting badly; Anderson and Cameron are happy together) and just knit. Knit one stitch after the other on a mindless two-row-repeated-pattern lace shawl with the sweetest, softest yarn in shades of blue and green. I chose one of Sue's products, and I have fun imagining which of her scary sheep she had to shear to produce it. *K3. yo. Knit to marker. yo. K1. yo. Knit to last 3 sts. yo. K3 ...*

The front door opens and I hear a familiar voice say, "Hello, Rowan. Hi, Pat."

Mrs. Bart. I look up and wave hello.

"Hi, Bliss. Ooooh, that looks lovely." She eyes my work in progress. "I might have to get you to put together a kit for me."

"No problem at all," says Mom. "It's some of Sleepy Sheep Sue's yarn. Isn't it gorgeous?"

Yes, that is the name of Sue's farm: Sleepy Sheep. And yes, Mrs. Bart, and anyone who comes into our store regularly, knows about Sue.

"Gorgeous." She comes over to take a closer look. I stop knitting and spread it out on the table so she can see it better. "Doesn't that knit up beautifully?" She takes it between the fingers of one hand and gently rubs a section between her fingers.

"How's Sydney doing?" I ask. "She wasn't at school yesterday."

Mrs. Bart drops the knitting and sits down so we can talk together quietly. No need to share the story of the pregnant granddaughter with the rest of String Theory.

"She just seems very tired and down," Mrs. Bart says. "So many appointments, so many people advising her and preparing her." She glances at me to see if I know what she's talking about. I do. Sydney has told me about the midwives (Sharlene is nice; Margo is all business) and the social worker, and all the papers that have to be read, explained, and signed. ("It feels like applying to university," she told me a week ago.)

I just nod, and Mrs. Bart nods back.

"I'm sure the next few weeks are going to be hard," she says. "So anything you can do to support her would be very much appreciated, Bliss."

Hard for Sydney, but hard for her, too, I think.

"Of course. We all kind of keep an eye on her," I say, and that makes her smile.

"She was exhausted after staying late for the volleyball game the other night. You'd think she was the one out on the floor," she says.

"Well, she was cheering pretty energetically for Anderson, and ..."

The door opens again, bringing another wave of cold November air. And Finn Nordin. Eye lock, just for a second, and then I notice he's not alone.

"Hello, Ava," says Mom in her most welcoming voice. "Hi, Finn. Nice to see you both."

"Hi," he says, and glances over at me again. "Uh, Ava needed to see Bliss about something."

"Help Desk is open for business." Mom waves them in my direction and they head over.

"I'll leave you to your friends, Bliss," Mrs. Bart stands up, smiles at me. "Thanks, dear."

"Oh, okay. You're welcome."

I'm not sure why she's thanking me, since I didn't really offer any help. But maybe just talking about Sydney helps. Maybe that "we all kind of keep an eye on her" comment helped. I'll text Sydney later and see how she's doing ...

And all this is going through my mind as Finn and Ava approach and I try not to look at him. Which is hard, because I want to look at him. But instead, I focus on Ava.

Ava, who does not look happy.

"Hi," I say. "It's nice to see you."

"Hi."

The two of them stop by the table and there's an awkward waiting moment. Okay.

"So, have you been working on your scarf? Or maybe your cat blankets? I haven't seen you for a while." I pull out the chair next to me. "Here, sit down."

She sits and unzips her coat. Finn stays standing, as if thinking about it, and then pulls out the chair across from me and sits down, too.

"I finished the scarf. And I have one cat blanket almost done, but it doesn't have a face on it. Just a plain blue colour," she says. It sounds like a homework report rather than something she's excited about.

Something is off here.

"Well, that's great," I say and, because I can't think of anything better, I pick up my shawl and start stitching again. Fill the silence and provide a bit of entertainment until she figures out what she wants to say to me.

"Wow, you're fast," says Finn.

I look at him then, and he's half-smiling at me, and the one thing I notice isn't the blue, blue eyes, or the tiny scar (well, okay, maybe I do notice those), but that he looks exhausted. Like someone who hasn't slept.

So, just as he's looking at me with what seems to be a "Sorry, I've been kind of out of it" smile, and I'm looking at him with a "What's up?" smile, Ava says:

"Can I donate my cat blanket to the club you and Finn are in?"

Snap back to reality, and this moment, and the little girl sitting beside me who, I now notice, looks as if she hasn't slept much either.

"That would be very kind of you," I say. "Of course you can."

A little smile creeps up on her. She's adorable. "Really?"

"Of course. And if you bring it to me, or have your brother bring it in, we'll display your cat blanket at our Clubs Showcase at school, too."

"Really?" She's almost smiling now.

"Sure. And I'll make sure your name is added to the list," I tell her. Then, brilliant idea: "In fact, I'm going to make sure we have a sign that says the cat blankets with the faces on them were created by Ava Nordin."

Now she's beaming at me.

"Your name should be there, too," she says. I love this. A kid who believes in fair play. "You helped make the pattern."

251

"But you invented it and did the first draft, so ..."

"So, co-creators," says Finn, and joins the three-way beamfest. "That's great, eh, Ava?"

I feel as if I just gave her the best present ever. When my eyes meet his, I could swear he's saying something along the lines of *Thank you. She needed this today.*

"Yay." She hugs herself, and then turns to Finn. "You said I could get some more yarn."

"I did." He looks over his shoulder at the displays and aisles behind him. "Why don't you go have a look around and see what catches your eye. Do you need help?"

"No. I'll call you if I need help." She shrugs out of her jacket and heads straight over to a display of rainbow-dyed worsted over by the counter.

Mom sees her coming and leans over: "Don't you just love this?"

And while they're focused on their mutual yarn worship, Finn turns back to me and says quickly, and in a voice no one else can hear: "Thanks for this. I had to distract her with something." He pauses, swallows. I just wait. (Help Desk Pro Tip: Wait for it. I know when someone needs to talk, and he has *that look.*) "My parents are having the worst fight ever and I just wanted to get out of the house. She was pretty upset."

"I'm so sorry."

Parents. Fighting. Mall. Coffee shop ... Yikes.

"Yeah, thanks." He glances back at Ava to make sure she's occupied, and then looks back. "Something's going on. Don't know what. But I needed to get out of the house, too." He shrugs. "So, yay for the Help Desk."

"Always ready to help," I say, and I hope he knows I mean more than knitting.

"Thanks."

And the way he says it, the way he looks at me, tells me that he absolutely knows. Oh, dear.

This is the thought that goes through my mind: *So, are Karlee and Taz a thing now?*

Followed by: *Stop it, Bliss!*

"Can I get this one, Finn?" Ava calls from the counter. She has one of the big, colourful skeins in her hand, and is waving it in the air while Mom grins at her, very mom-like.

"Sure. Sure, you can." He pushes back his chair and stands up. "So, are you ready for the math contest?"

This week. Monday. Final instructions arrived in our inboxes this morning.

"I so am."

And we grin at each other. Yarn, knitting, happy little sister, math contest teammates. Order restored.

For now.

46. WALK IN THE PARK

Text from Sydney on Sunday morning:

Hey. Walk by the river?

She's already sitting on our bench when I get there, hunched in on herself, arms folded over her bump, which is really more of a bulge now. The puffy parka makes her look even more impressive. The red scarf (hand-knitted! I recognize that yarn from 3C Club) wrapped several times around her neck, and Canada toque on her head just add to the overall impression of someone trying to hide under layers of winter clothing.

Her eyes are on the river, still flowing despite the dropping temperatures, but she nods as I sit down beside her.

"Hey," she says.

"Hey."

I wait and watch the water. It doesn't take long.

"So, I hear Finn Nordin came to visit you at the store yesterday."

Okay, I did not see that coming. I should have, I guess. Mrs. Bart, teller of tales.

"Well, actually, he brought his sister to see me."

"Right."

I glance over and she's grinning.

"He brought his sister because ..." and I stop, because it doesn't seem like a good idea to tell Sydney about the messy Nordin Family Saga now underway.

"Because?"

"She was having a bad day and he knows about the healing power of yarn now, so he brought her in to buy some."

"Right," she says again. "Yarn."

Time to shut this down.

"It's cold just sitting here. Want to walk?" Movement is always good for conversations. The movement of hands on needles, yarn slipping through fingers, or the movement of feet on a path. Doesn't matter.

Sydney agrees, apparently, because she hauls herself to her feet, hands still in her pockets, and says, "Sure. Let's go."

And once we're moving, she starts, exactly as I knew she would.

"So, I had an email from Magnus."

Ah. Magnus.

I'm actually a bit relieved, because after Mrs. Bart's concern

255

yesterday, I thought I might be in for a conversation about pregnancy, and pre-delivery jitters, and technical, body things that I really, really don't want to hear about. (But, of course, being a good friend and experienced Help Desk pro, I would listen to without letting on my discomfort.)

But this is a relief. New developments about Magnus Haugen, I can take.

"Really? Good or bad email?"

She doesn't say anything for a few minutes, so we just walk. And then a big sigh.

"Good, I guess. He apologized for being a jerk the last time he wrote." She shrugs. "Doesn't change anything, though."

"Apologies are good."

"They are," she says. "He's still a jerk, though."

Her voice is ... tired. Weary. Of course, carrying an ever-increasing bulge around all day and night, as well as living with the upcoming fun of labour and delivery, must be exhausting. And possibly terrifying. Although Sydney has never shown fear, at least, not to me. But who knows? She's missed more school in the last three weeks than she has since September. Something's up, and it may just be the lingering shadow of Magnus Haugen.

"So, what did he say?"

We're walking through a park, near a deserted playground now. In summer, this place is a zoo of kids running around and climbing and swinging. Having fun. Making noise. Bethany and Anderson and I played here a million years ago when nothing mattered but sunshine and where the next snack was coming from. Today, it just looks sad, deserted, and cold.

"He said he was sorry about what he said. That he's sorry *this* happened." She takes one red-mittened hand out of her pocket and waves it at her bulge. "That he hopes I'm okay and will be back curling next season."

"Wow."

"I know, eh?" she almost laughs at that. Not a happy laugh, but a sort of snort. "As if I wouldn't be curling next season. As if he thinks I'm going to be home, taking care of this baby."

We walk a few more steps and the path winds closer to the flowing river. I love this sound. A steady, solid burble. It sounds cold, if that's possible.

"But you're not, right?"

There's a pause, long enough to make me look over at her. A few weeks ago, she told me a bit about her meeting with the social worker: all the paperwork, all the questions she got to ask about how they choose the people who will eventually raise this baby. No emotion, just cool and business-like. But right now, she doesn't sound business-like.

"No," she says, finally. "I'm giving it up for adoption."

"Okay."

We come to another bench, perched on the snowy grass beside the river, and she plops herself down on it and stares at the water.

"It's pretty clear he doesn't want anything to do with any of this, which means, I'm on my own." She slumps back. "It's all under control. Family and Children Services. Midwives. Everybody knows the plan. Including me. Baby arrives, baby goes, I finish the semester and go home. Sounds easy."

I look over at her, and she's staring at the river, only now her eyes are brimming with tears.

"It's not easy," I say.

She continues to stare at the water. And then, just as I'm starting to think about suggesting we start walking again because I'm freezing, she takes a huge, shuddering breath, looks over at me and says,

"I wish I'd never told him."

47. MATH CONTEST: PART ONE

I don't know what's going on. Something is very, very wrong here.

We're in the van, on our way to Waterloo, and the only word Finn has said to me so far this morning is, "Shotgun." This, after an awkwardly silent few minutes of hanging out in front of the main office waiting for Wenzik to arrive.

Awkward, because Finn came walking toward me, phone out and earbuds in, and when I smiled at him and said, "Hi," he just nodded, unsmiling, sat down on the bench, and started scrolling. Eyes on his phone. Ignoring me.

Odd. A bit more than odd. Maybe scary. My face is hot, my hands are cold, and I just stand there, looking at him, until I realize he is completely ignoring me on purpose. I go stand at the glass doors and look out at a dull November morning and try to problem solve.

But this is not a complicated math question or a challenging new stitch, and I don't quite know where to start. Something is keeping me from thinking straight, and that is not a great state of being on the day of a high-profile inter-school math competition ... just saying.

"Okay, guys. Ready?" Wenzik comes out of the office with his backpack and the van keys, smiling at us on his way to the door. "Let's go."

Which is when Finn, following me out the door, says "Shotgun," and passes me on the way to the school's minivan, parked along the front walk.

Fine. Whatever. I climb into the back seat and feel frozen, while Finn sits silently in the front seat with Wenzik, who is being teacherly and hasn't seemed to notice any weirdness.

"Okay guys, registration desk and ID, then a little meet-and-greet. Muffins and juice. Was there coffee and tea for you guys last year, Bliss? I can't remember." He catches my eye in the rear-view mirror and I manage to shrug. "Anyway, they feed us something. Then we go to whatever room we're assigned to and find our table. And then, it's on!"

He makes it sound like the start of the Stanley Cup playoffs and probably expects us to jump in and be suitably excited, so our silence catches him a little. He looks over at Finn, looks at me again in the rear-view mirror.

"Hey, don't be nervous, guys." He uses his best teacher-coach voice. "You're going to do great."

Okay. This is stupid. Somebody has to step up here and, clearly, it's not going to be Finn.

"Yeah, we know. Thanks. Hey, Mr. Wenzik?" I say, going for a little deflection. "Do you know what other schools are going to be there? Will that annoying school with the cranky teacher from last year be there again?"

And that gives him something to talk about as we cruise down the highway toward the university, me sitting, not really listening, shivering and jumpy and confused in the backseat. Finn, silent and staring out the side window, in the front.

Clearly, we are off to a great start.

48. MATH CONTEST: PART TWO

We're in first place, which is astonishing.

Or maybe not. Since Finn isn't talking to me, except for strictly math-problem interchanges—*if x equals 2, then y equals 5*—we are completely focused on the work and not on each other or this weird dynamic that has suddenly sprung up between us. So I've slipped into a rhythm, into the zone and, after a while, he's just another source of information, rather than the boy I connected with two days ago at the String Theory Help Desk. Or the boy who stood with me on the dark sidewalk outside The Beanbag.

Or the boy I danced with at the Not Halloween Dance.

But I'm not going there.

Nope, I'm sunk so deep into Math World, and so zeroed in on the final problem that needs to be solved before that annoyingly snobby duo from, yes, the annoying school, figures it out, that

I might as well be here alone. Fifteen minutes have gone by (I think fifteen minutes have gone by. Quick check of the clock. Yes, fifteen minutes have gone by) since he last said anything to me, which was "Modulo, right?" *Of course, modulo.*

And then, just as I finish writing the last line of the proof and lift my pencil off the page, he says, "Okay. Look, Bliss. Listen."

It takes me a moment to realize he just said something real and not math related. At first, I don't even look up at him. But then the math fog clears and I do.

"What?"

He's looking at me, not smiling, not anything. Of course his timing is terrible. I'm not ready to climb out of the zone yet because there's still first place to consider, after all.

"Is this right?" I tap the answer I just wrote on the problem page, and now it's his turn to recalibrate.

"Uh, let's see." He leans over and traces through the proof with his pencil. "I think so."

"Okay. I'm submitting it then."

"Bliss," he says, just as I flick on the light that tells the officials we've got an answer to submit. "Why didn't you tell me?"

49. YOU TOLD

We're at the post-event social. If you can even call it that. Really, it's just a bunch of high school students standing around in the foyer of some big university building, eating donuts (or hummus and crackers for anyone avoiding sugar, but probably that's never going to happen), drinking juice, and recovering from a day of fun with math.

Fun if you win, that is. And we did. That pair from our arch-rivals was very disappointed, but good sports. Their teacher, not so much.

"She *is* in Grade 11, right?" the cranky teacher said to Wenzik, not smiling, as we stood waiting to go up and get our trophy. "I remember her from last year."

"She sure is," he smiled back.

So, the presentation is done and we're supposed to be mingling with the other competitors, sharing math stories, maybe, or commiserating over that really hard probability question about whether the box has a gold marble or a black marble. (The answer was D, 7/30.)

Finn and I are not mingling. Not even with each other, even though we're standing together near the stairs, a little apart from the action. Wenzik was with us for a while, but we are not fun, so he's gone off to visit with some of his math teacher friends. I can see him downing another donut—maybe his third?—and laughing with his colleagues. The cranky teacher from the second-place school isn't in the group.

We haven't said a word to each other since the end of the contest, when I hit the light just as he asked his question, just as the judges sprang into action, just as our opponents sagged back into their seats in disappointment, just as the score was read out and they announced our names and Central as the winners. Just as it got loud and busy, and we were pulled along into the whole end-of-contest circus. Even afterwards, when Wenzik shook our hands and was clearly ready to celebrate, and then looked at each of us in turn, trying to figure out why we weren't jumping up and down in triumph. *Teenagers,* I could read the speech bubble over his head. And he went off to hang out with his friends. Just like a teenager.

So, Finn and me. Standing by the stairs.

Why didn't you tell me?

Time to solve this problem.

"Why didn't I tell you what?"

I just throw it out there, hoping it's not what I think it is, but knowing it is. When he doesn't answer right away, I take a quick glance at him. His mouth is in a straight line, eyes a bit squinty, and fixed on something far away, maybe on the other side of the foyer, maybe way beyond that. His house, maybe, and the people in it.

He's silent for so long that I think he's not going to answer. And then, in a voice that makes me go hot and cold in the same moment, without looking at me, mouth hardly moving as he spits the words out:

"I told you about my parents fighting. Way back, that night we were at the café. And then Saturday, with Ava. I told you something was up. And you knew. You knew what my mother was doing. You knew about it, and you told—I'm guessing Adele? And now everything's a mess. And you could have told me. It would have helped to know. And you knew. And you could have told me. You should have told me."

I'm trying to follow this logically. Yes, he told me about his parents fighting. Yes, he told me something was up at home and Ava needed my Help Desk help. Yes, I knew about his stupid mother and her stupid boyfriend. But ...

You told. And what about that Adele part?

266

I haven't told anyone.

"I—I didn't—" I start, but he cuts me off. Raises his hand.

"My little sister's a mess. My parents are screaming at each other. And my mother says to me, 'Thank your little knitting friend for me,' before she slams out of the house this morning."

He turns and looks at me then.

"I thought we were friends. I thought ..." He swallows, never takes his eyes off me. I'm frozen, trying to work this out. *I didn't tell anyone. How could I tell you?* "I thought maybe more than that. You should have told me."

And then he walks away.

50. SLEEPWALKING

So, it's a long week, and I'm not sure I'm fully awake for much of it. Mostly I'm trying to avoid meeting Finn in the hallway at school. Until I figure this out.

Monday night, when they get home from String Theory, I show off my medal to Mom and Dad, tell them the contest was fantastic but I am *soooo* exhausted, and retreat to bed early, where I distract myself by texting with Bethany about her growing doubts that James is The One.

He's ghosting me. Hey! Taz and Karlee are a thing!

Ghost him back. T & K wow.

Wow, for sure. Maybe that's another reason Finn was so mad today? His girlfriend dumped him?

I thought maybe more than that …

Bethany doesn't seem to be in bad shape over James, though, so I let her text on, and finally plead exhaustion after my big day of solving math problems, and sign off.

On Tuesday, Finn and I have to stand up during assembly so everyone can clap loudly at our math contest win. We're on opposite sides of the auditorium, so it's fine. I glance over at him but he doesn't look at me.

"All right, all right," Mrs. DeLello, the principal, smiles and holds up a hand to calm Finn's jock buddies who are getting into full championship-trophy-presentation mode and taking it a bit too far with the whooping.

Anderson, Sydney, and Bethany throw out a couple of whoops of their own—"Yay, Bliss!"—in support, which I appreciate.

But mostly I'm sleepwalking through the day. Going to class, keeping my eyes on my desk, my books, my laptop. Letting Sydney and Bethany carry the conversation at lunch. Avoiding Anderson's eyes when he leans over while the girls are distracted by something on Bethany's phone, and asks me, "You okay?"

I nod, once, and smile a small, tight little smile. All I can manage. He knows I'm not okay, so he smiles the same smile back at me, and that helps.

I make it through Tuesday. More texting with Bethany on Tuesday night.

James says he wants to take a break. Jerk

Sorry

It's ok. Tired of dealing with him.

Good attitude

What's up with you and Finn??????

Nothing

Right

Long pause, and I'm relieved she doesn't dig for more. Then,

Let me know if you want to talk

I break my rule and send her a heart emoji. She replies with:

Boys are such a pain

We then start a chat with Anderson and Sydney about the upcoming 3C Club booth (which is, in fact, just a table) at the Clubs Showcase this Saturday in the school gym. Charis has a figure-skating competition (this girl, honestly, does it all) so I'm in charge, with my trusty team of volunteers. And thank goodness I have them, because it's not easy to organize an event like this when you're as out of it as I am.

And I am so out of it.

Why didn't you tell me? You told. You told. You told ...

I thought maybe more than that ...

But I'm not going there. Not looking ahead any further than Saturday afternoon.

Wednesday morning I tell Mom I think I'm coming down with a cold.

"Can I stay home and try to sleep it off?" I try to look pathetic, which isn't hard, because I do actually feel pathetic.

"Of course, honey," she feels my forehead (which is cool, of course, because I am not coming down with a cold) and then puts her hands on either side of my face and smiles at me. "Go sleep it off. Drink tea. Watch movies. Take a 'me' day. You need it."

She pulls me in for a hug and I wish I could stay here all day. I wish we could stay here all day. Mothers—well, my mother.

Why didn't you tell me?

So Wednesday is a lost day. I don't even return texts until the evening, when I should be helping Mom at Knit & Natter but, well, that's not going to happen.

Feeling better? Bethany and Anderson.

Yup.

Nothing from Sydney.

At 3C Club on Thursday (yes, I'm back at it), Charis and I organize all the donations and get everyone to make individual posters introducing themselves so we can display creations with their creators. Finn, Karlee, and Adele do not appear, but I make a special poster for Ava's cat blankets, including her name as co-creator of the cat-face design. (I've done three of them. They're awesome.)

And it's only when I'm at my locker at the end of the day that I get the text from Sydney:

At the hospital. This is it. Wish me luck.

51. NEWS

"Thanks for letting us know, Jeannette. Yes, I'll tell Bliss." Mom pauses, glances over at me, smiling. "Okay. And please let us know if you need anything. No problem. Bye."

Friday night at String Theory. The store is empty of shoppers, with closing time minutes away. Just Dad, Mom, and me, all at the front counter. Dad has his arm around me as we lean there, listening to Mom talk to Mrs. Bart.

It's dark outside the store window, and snowflakes are drifting down. Across the street, I can see the lights of The Beanbag. A couple at the front window are standing up and reaching for their coats. Closing time there soon, too. The Beanbag. Me and Finn at The Beanbag ...

Mom hangs up and turns to us. Sighs.

"It's a boy," she says. A smile, but it's a sad smile. "Sydney's fine. Her parents are with her now."

A baby boy. I wonder if he has dark hair and looks like Magnus Haugen, but of course I don't say that out loud.

"Jeanette's okay?" asks Dad.

"I think so." Mom shrugs. "Worried about them all. Sad for them, I think. Sad for herself, too." They look at each other, and I know they're thinking about the arrival of their baby, and what a big thing that was. She looks at me. "But all is well."

I don't tell them this is old news to me.

That was brutal but I'm ok, Sydney texted me this afternoon during my spare, as I sat in the library, tucked into a study carrel with my earbuds in, streaming a World Music playlist and browsing Ravelry for small-animal crochet patterns. (Okay, yes, I was hiding.)

Glad you're ok.

I don't ask, but she tells me anyway.

A boy

Something about those two words make it real. Not a bump to be stared at, or a conversation over email with some jerk Norwegian curling boy.

Thinking of you

That was hours ago, and I haven't heard anything since. I'm sure Mrs. Bart has been at the hospital all day, and now Sydney's parents. They're probably gathered in her room, I hope being kind and supportive. I bet it's excruciating.

"Well, let's pack up and get home," says Dad, and Mom sighs again and deals with the cash, while he goes down the hallway to shut off the lights and grab their coats.

I retrieve my coat and backpack from the Help Desk table and pull out my phone.

Need anything?

I don't expect to hear anything, but after a moment, the little bubble shows me she's typing something.

A visit. Need to see a face that isn't a disappointed adult.

Sure!! When?

Now?

52. SYDNEY

Dad drops Mom and me at the hospital and goes to wait in the car, while Mom makes sure I can go in.

"You're not family, Bliss," she says. "And it's probably past visiting hours. They might not let you in."

But of course, Mrs. Bart is there, and Sydney's parents, and when Sydney tells them they have to let me in, Mrs. Bart comes down to meet us.

"She'd love to see you, Bliss," she says. "Go on up. Fourth floor, turn left. Nursing station is right there and they know you're coming."

They do. A nurse smiles at me when I ask at the desk— "You're Sydney's friend. Room 403, just down the hall, see it? Her mom's at the door"—and I see a tall woman who could be Sydney's twin standing at the door, watching for me, waving.

"Hi, you must be Bliss," she says as I approach. "Thanks for coming, dear. I know Sydney will really appreciate a visit."

And then she leads the way into the room.

I'm not sure why I'm nervous, but I am. I've been nervous all the way here in the car, going up in the elevator. *Don't look too far ahead,* I keep telling myself. *One stitch at a time.*

I just don't know what I'm going to find waiting for me.

"Hey."

She's sitting up in bed and looks absolutely normal. Not like a sixteen-year-old Grade 11 student who just gave birth to a baby. Not tired. Not in pain. Just kind of bored, as if she was plunked out of class, told to put on a hospital gown, and climb into this bed for a while.

Is it wrong to admit that I feel a moment of relief? I'm not sure what I was expecting, but I should have known better. Sydney is just fine.

Until she smiles at me, and then I see it.

I want to get this thing out of me and get my body and my life back. That's what she said back in September, that first day she joined Bethany and Anderson and me for lunch. That day we beat Cameron and Peter at badminton.

It's just not quite that easy.

"Well, I'll leave you two to visit for a few minutes, okay, love?" Sydney's mother says, coming over to kiss her on the head. They hug gently, and smile at each other, and with a last pat on her daughter's shoulder, and a smile at me, her mom walks out and Sydney meets my eyes.

"This might be the first time in over a year that my mother and I have actually gotten along so great," she says with a half-laugh, before wincing and rearranging herself a little in the bed. "Without yelling at each other."

I come over and sit on the chair beside the bed and we grin at each other.

"That's nice, isn't it?" I say. "You and your mom? Like a team?"

"Yeah, I guess." She shrugs. "Thanks for coming. I just needed to see someone who isn't thinking, *Oh poor teenage girl with the baby*." She shifts herself a little. Grimaces. "You're not thinking that, right?"

"Nope, not what I'm thinking."

She narrows her eyes at me. "Okay, then. What are you thinking?"

"I'm thinking how great you look," I say. "Like you're ready to jump out of this bed and take on Cameron and Peter in another badminton game."

That makes her laugh. And wince again.

"No, no, I'm not quite ready for that." But she smiles at the thought, at least. "They're keeping me overnight, just to be sure all the parts are doing what the parts are supposed to do."

I don't want details and I think she knows it, but she adds:

277

"The parts took a bit of a beating."

Okay, enough of this. Time for a subject change.

"So, you and your mom seem to be good."

"Yeah." She looks down at her hands, folded across what remains of the bump. "We've been talking about—about next steps."

Something in her voice catches me.

"Next steps?"

"My mom and I have been talking about keeping him," she says.

Keeping the baby. Taking this baby boy back to Ottawa and raising him. A single mother, age sixteen.

She lifts her eyes to mine and we look at each other for a long, silent moment.

"Mom says we'll do whatever I want to do. She says they'll be there to help me, if that's what I want."

Why do I feel like I just turned on my Help Desk sign ...?

"Is that what you want?" I ask.

"Right now, I don't know what I want." Her voice breaks.

So I get up from the chair and slide in beside her on the bed, gently, so I don't disturb her sore parts, until we're arm to arm, shoulder to shoulder, squished side by side on the hospital bed, both of us staring at the opposite wall with its painting of a seashore, a lighthouse. (In a birthing unit? You would expect bunny pictures or something, wouldn't you?)

She lets her head sink down onto my shoulder and I can just look down my nose and see her mouth as she speaks. Her lips tremble.

"I want to keep him," she whispers.

"Okay," I whisper back.

"But I won't." Her voice is getting shaky. "Because I can't give him the life a baby needs. A teenage mother who's still in high school, and no dad."

Yes. Especially a dad whose first reaction was to run in the other direction.

"I don't know how I would do it." Her voice is getting shaky. "I'd probably be a crap mother. It would be the stupidest, worst thing I've ever done."

Not stupider than having sex with a guy named Magnus who is on the other side of the world and couldn't care less about you. Of course, I don't say this out loud.

Instead, I take her hand in mine and give it a squeeze. Like my mom does. And Auntie Bryn. Like Dad does. Anderson. When I need someone else there, someone to attach to.

We sit there, snuggled up together for a minute, and then I take a quick glance and see the tears on her cheeks. I squeeze her hand again and she gives a nod, eyes closed.

"Thanks, Bliss," she whispers back.

53. CAT BLANKETS

"These are adorable!" gushes the lady with the giant crocheted shoulder bag. I'm pretty sure I've seen her at String Theory once or twice, but she doesn't recognize me.

She's leaning over the three squares with their cat faces stitched right into the pattern, just as Ava designed them.

"Designed by this little girl, Ava Nordin," I say, pointing at the stand-up poster I've strategically positioned nearby. "They're going to be donated to the Humane Society."

The lady looks up then and says, "Well, dear, I'm sure you could sell these. Easily. Cat people would love them. I love them."

Maybe Ava and I could open an Etsy shop and make a killing. Sadly, this would involve communicating with Ava and her family, which is highly unlikely, since the last words her brother and I exchanged were six days ago. And I don't expect many words to be exchanged in the future.

But I'm putting that behind me, because whatever Finn Nordin may think of me, I know I didn't do anything wrong. I just wish we could talk about it.

But no. It's done. Over. Whenever I see him at school, he's with his jock friends (not Karlee, not Adele, who have now formed a neat little foursome with Taz and James), his gaze anywhere but in my direction.

"You're too good for him," Anderson whispered in my ear at lunch yesterday, when he caught me glancing over my shoulder toward a certain corner of the lunchroom.

"No," I whispered back. "It was just an unsolvable equation."

Anderson is here beside me, at the Crafting for Community Care Club table in the gym, sharing hosting duties with me and Bethany. And we are rocking it. There has been a steady flow of students, parents, visitors from the community—like cat lady with the crocheted shoulder bag—and even some of our donation organizations.

"We'll take all of them," the man from the Welcome Centre said, nodding at the multicoloured pile of K2 P2 woollen scarves. "And thank you. Great work, and very much appreciated."

The lady from the local hospital's volunteer organization was just as excited about an impressive pile of baby blankets and preemie hats that Bethany, Anderson, and I whipped up over the past few weeks.

We send a selfie to Sydney, who let me know she got home from the hospital around lunchtime and is crashed in front of the TV at her grandmother's house, watching movies with her mom and drinking hot chocolate.

My team, she texts back.

Cameron is at the super-busy floor-hockey booth—they take up three tables—down the aisle and across from us, and I see him and Anderson sending signs to each other. Mostly smiles.

"You're too good for him," I say to Anderson, and he grins.

"Maybe."

It doesn't matter, though, because I don't know if I've ever seen Anderson this happy. He keeps flinging an arm around my shoulders and squeezing me, as if I'm his favourite stuffed toy.

I love it.

"Can't I just buy one?" A Grade 9 girl is now admiring the cat blankets, too. Really, I think we're on to something here.

"No, sorry," says Bethany. "These are all for donation. But," she looks over and catches my eye, "maybe you could join 3C Club next term and Bliss here will teach you how to make your own?"

Bethany, the ultimate salesperson. She's cool, efficient, and clearly completely over the brief romance with James.

"So over him," she tells me, giving a little fling of her hand, like whisking away an annoying insect. "Have you seen that cool Grade 12 guy in the mountain biking club? I think his name's Shane."

Bethany will be fine. She and I are planning to get together tonight, kick her brothers out of the rec room (they can watch the hockey game up in the family room), and do our first *Love, Actually* viewing of the pre-Christmas season. We usually watch it anywhere from six to ten times in the weeks leading up to the holidays (and sometimes beyond) and, as Bethany says, "I think we need it this year."

So everyone is happy, and everything is fine. And then ...

"My cat blankets! Look, Dad!"

I had been looking down the table at Bethany and her sales job, so the voice catches me by surprise.

Ava.

Her sweet little face is lit up with excitement, and she's looking up at the man standing beside her, who leans over to see them more closely.

"Hi, Bliss!" She smiles at me. "This is my dad."

Mr. Nordin, the husband whose wife is behaving badly.

But apparently, whatever is going on in this family isn't being carried out into the wide world, because he smiles at me and says, "Oh, Finn's math contest partner."

Okay.

I smile, polite, not sure exactly where this is going. "Hi, yes. Math."

"Math and knitting," says Ava. "Like me."

"Exactly," laughs her dad and we all smile at each other.

"Hey, and me, too."

Someone has stepped up into the scene and is now standing beside Ava. She looks up at him and laughs. I just keep my eyes on her because I have absolutely no idea what to expect.

"Like you, too!" Ava says. "Right, Bliss?"

"Right." I glance up at him, not sure what I'm going to find.

He's there, those blue eyes and that tiny little scar. Not smiling, exactly, but not straight-mouthed, angry, distant, like the last time I saw him this close.

"Hey."

"Hey."

Mr. Nordin has moved down the table and is now admiring the poster with Ava's name on it, and Bethany, with a glance my way, jumps in.

"Isn't this fabulous? Ava, you're a star." She glances at me again, widens her eyes meaningfully, and keeps them talking. Distraction 101.

Which means Finn and I are now face to face across the table.

"Can you get away for a few minutes?" he asks me. "Go for a walk outside or something?"

What? What?

"Um, I guess."

I look over at Bethany, who's still talking with Ava and her dad. Then I feel a touch on my shoulder and Anderson's voice, "Go. I've got this." And he's pushing me gently toward the space at the end of the table. "Hi, Finn. How's it going?"

The two boys nod at each other and I feel very much as if I'm being managed.

"But ... okay," I start, as Anderson hands me my jacket and scarf.

"See you later," he says, and I look back and follow Finn toward the gym door, and the exit, and the bright sunshine of a Saturday afternoon in late November.

And Anderson, still smiling, doesn't even glance my way.

54. THE FIRST RULE OF KNITTING

"I'm sorry."

That's the first thing he says, and it's so unexpected, I almost stop walking.

"For what?"

Well, actually, I can think of a few things he might be sorry for, but I'm never sure anyone sees the world the same way I do.

"For acting like such a jerk," he says.

Okay.

We're walking along the sidewalk, jackets open, because the sun is mid-afternoon strong and there's hardly any wind. It feels like a chilly spring day, not November with the winter still ahead of us.

"You didn't act like a jerk," I say.

"I did," he says. "Nice of you to say that, though."

We walk some more and, although I'm pretty sure we're

headed toward a conversation about his mother, and what I heard in the dark hallway at String Theory, I have no idea how we're going to get there.

Don't look too far ahead ...

But he takes it all out of my hands by asking, "So, you knew, didn't you? About my mother? Why didn't you tell me my mother was having an affair with some guy?"

He's not angry. When I glance at him, he looks back at me and shrugs. His mouth quirks up in an almost-grin.

"They had it out last night, finally. Big fight, followed by big cry, followed by big conversation, followed by big, I don't know, truce." He looks over at me. "That would be my parents, I mean."

"Oh." Yikes. Glad this didn't take place in a dark hallway at String Theory. "That must have been hard for you. And Ava."

"Yeah, it was. But it was good, too, because we finally found out what all the shit was, what's been going on in our family for the past few months."

We walk along for a few minutes.

"Parents," he says. "Or, at least, *my* parents. Yours seem pretty cool."

I have never, ever, loved my parents more than I do at this moment and immediately send them a telepathic giant hug.

"They are. Cool. The best," I say, because it's not bragging if it's true, right?

287

"So, why didn't you tell me? About my mom, I mean. You had lots of chances." He doesn't sound angry, just curious. Maybe even confused.

"I don't know," I say. "I thought about it, many times."

Are you kidding? I thought about it constantly. Practically every time I was with him.

"Okay," he says. "But ...?"

"But, I just couldn't." I shrug. "I thought it might be too ... hard. Too embarrassing. Or hurt you. Or hurt Ava."

He just stares down at the sidewalk, walking and nodding.

"I almost told you, at the dance, remember?" I glance at him and he looks over at me, thinking. I wonder if he remembers that moment the way I do. Right after we danced together.

"Right, I do remember that," he says, looking back down at the sidewalk. I can't tell what he's thinking.

"But I didn't have a chance. And then I just hoped it would go away," I try to explain. "Like, if I stayed out of it. I was a coward, I guess."

We walk in silence and I have no idea if this explanation works for him or not. But I realize it's exactly the truth. Telling doesn't always work. Keeping secrets doesn't work, either, but telling him about his mother—

"But I'm not sorry," I glance at him. "Maybe I should have told you. Maybe you could have helped your parents, I don't know. I

288

don't know your family well enough to know. But I just couldn't. I'm sorry if you were hurt. Or Ava. But I just couldn't tell."

"You don't have to be sorry," he says.

He stops, reaches out for my arm, and turns me so that we're facing each other. "Not telling me. Thinking you were protecting me and Ava. It was kind of you." And then he shakes his head. "I was the jerk, getting mad at you like that, the day of the contest."

Ah. The part of this whole thing I don't understand.

"Okay, at the math contest," I say. "You asked why I didn't tell you. And you said something about Adele. Why would I ever tell Adele anything? I mean, she hates me, right?"

"Yeah, Adele," he says, closing his eyes for a moment, the way you do when you're trying to block out a bad moment from the murky past. Then he opens them again and sighs. "It turns out, Adele saw Mom with some guy at Northfield Mall, and told her mom, who told my dad, and the shit hit the fan."

Adele stomping through the mall that day, looking annoyed ...

"It wasn't you who made this whole thing blow up," he says. "It was Adele. Mom yelled something about why didn't I just ask my little knitting friend, and I just assumed you'd spilled it to Adele. Because I told you she was my cousin." He shakes his head again, as if he's trying to solve a math problem. "But you didn't, did you?"

The stitches fall into place, one after the other, row on row.

I take a deep breath and go for it.

"Okay, this is what happened. I heard your mother talking to someone on the phone, in the hallway at String Theory. I didn't even know who she was then, but she mentioned your name. And then another time, in the hallway—I think she was talking to him again."

Okay, I am NOT going to mention turned-down sheets and little packets. Not a chance.

"And then," I'm on a roll. It's just flowing out of me now, the *telling*. "She was in the store, picking up Ava that day, and my mom got talking about me and my hidden corner at the back during Knit & Natter. And your mom ..." I stop, remembering that awful moment. "I guess she figured it out then. Knew I had heard her. But I didn't tell anyone. Not even my parents. And never Adele."

He shakes his head and tries to smile. He mostly succeeds, but I can see it hurts. "Shit. My family. What a mess."

For a long moment we just stand there, and then he looks at me and he isn't smiling anymore. "But you and me. We're good. Right?"

His face. If this was Anderson or Bethany or Sydney standing across from me right now, I would be in there, hugging them so hard and saying, *Yes, of course we're good! It's going to be okay! And yes! We're always good!* But this is Finn Nordin, so I don't know ...

"Of course," I say with a nod. No hugging, though. "We're good."

And, as we stand there looking cautiously at each other, I realize we are good. We're very good. In fact, I don't think I've ever felt this kind of good before. I must tell Auntie Bryn tomorrow when she comes for Sunday supper.

"I guess we should get back?" he says, and he even manages a sort of smile.

"Sure. I guess we should."

Another moment of standing there in the sunshine, looking at each other, and then we turn back in the direction of the school and start walking.

He reaches over and takes my hand in his. I didn't know my hand was cold until I feel his fingers wrap around mine. His fingers are long, strong. Warm.

We walk. He squeezes my hand and I look up at him.

I expect him to say something. Or maybe I should say something? I don't know how this works. But then, this is all new to me. Maybe words aren't necessary here.

So, we just walk. Yes, Finn Nordin and I are walking along the sidewalk, holding hands.

I did not see that coming.

— The End —

KNITTING GUIDE FROM AUTHOR JEAN MILLS

Like Bliss Adair, I am a knitter. I have an impressive yarn stash, and at least three projects on the go at any time. Sitting with yarn and needles (or crochet hook) in my hands is relaxing, soothing, even meditative. So, maybe after reading this story about Bliss and the role knitting plays in her life, you might be inspired to give knitting a try, too. Here are three easy projects from the story to get you started.

But first, you'll need to learn these basic knitting stitches:

K	Knit
P	Purl
Kfb	Knit front and back (This is for increasing one stitch)
K2tog	Knit two stitches together (This is for decreasing one stitch)

Yo	Yarn over (This creates a space between stitches)
Cast on	
Cast off	(Sometimes called "bind off")

Take a look at a beginner knitting guide, or find an instructional video on YouTube, to help you learn these easy stitches.

3C CLUB SCARVES

Finn, Karlee, and Adele did, in fact, show up at 3C Club on Thursday and, as I wandered the room, helping the other knitters and checking in with Sydney, I watched as Anderson and Charis got them started on the K2 P2 scarf. Actually, Karlee started with a straight garter stitch knit-knit-knit scarf. She doesn't seem to have much fine motor skill prowess, but the yarn she chose (a fuzzy acrylic in a gorgeous shade of lilac) was perfect, so she's not without artistic vision, I believe. —Chapter 19, BLISS ADAIR AND THE FIRST RULE OF KNITTING

Note: Yarn for both scarf projects:

Pick at least a Medium (4) weight yarn for these scarf patterns. Read the label for suggested needle size. You'll need about 400–500 yards (450 metres) of yarn for a scarf 60 inches (150 cm) long.

1.3C Club Garter Stitch Scarf

Pattern:

Cast on 20 – 40 stitches (or more, for a wider scarf. Feel free to experiment!)

- Row 1: K to end of row
- Repeat Row 1 until the scarf is the length you want
- Cast off
- Weave in ends using a darning needle

2.3C Club Ribbed Scarf

Pattern:

Cast on 44 stitches (must be a multiple of 4)

- Row 1: *K2 (knit 2 stitches), P2 (purl 2 stitches). Repeat from * to end of row, ending with P2
- Repeat Row 1 until scarf is the length you want
- Cast off
- Weave in ends using a darning needle

BLISS'S KNITTING CURE BABY BLANKET

It's the simplest of all patterns, a baby blanket, knit on the diagonal. Mindless, but so satisfying, with its line of eyelet around the border, and the soft, variegated yarn that drifts from one pastel to the next without any effort. —Chapter 20,

BLISS ADAIR AND THE FIRST RULE OF KNITTING.

Yarn:

Use a Fine (3) weight yarn. There are lots of yarns intended specifically for baby projects. You'll need 800–1000 yards (730–915 metres). Use a set of circular needles (two needles attached by a long, flexible cable) to accommodate the width of the blanket. The yarn label will indicate which size of needle you need.

Pattern:

- Cast on 2 stitches
- Row 1: Knit

Increase:

- Row 1: K1, yo, K1
- Row 2: K2, yo, K1
- Row 3: K3, yo, K 1
- Row 4: K3, yo, K to end of row
- Repeat Row 4 until you have 160 stitches (or any size you wish)

Decrease:

- Row 1: K2, K2tog, yo, K2tog, K to end of row
- Repeat Row 1 until 4 stitches remain
- Next Row: K2tog twice (2 stitches remain on needle)
- Cast off
- Weave in ends using a darning needle

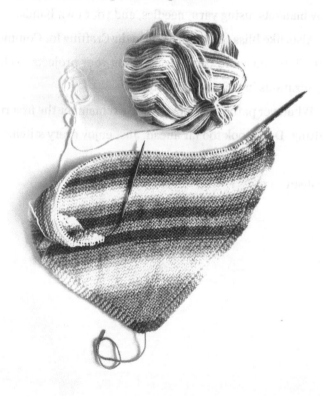

Final Note:

If these simple patterns draw you into the wonderful world of knitting, you can access lots of resources—books, magazines, online sites, helpful yarn shop employees—to help you find projects that might challenge you more. Or, keep it simple, and just enjoy the relaxing process of creating these easy scarves and baby blankets, using yarn, needles, and your own hands.

Also, like Bliss and her friends in the Crafting for Community Care Club, you could consider donating your projects to charity organizations in your community.

Whatever path you choose, always remember the first rule of knitting: Don't look too far ahead. Just enjoy every stitch.

Jean

ACKNOWLEDGMENTS

As always, I will start by saying that writing fiction is fun, because I get to make things up, but in writing Bliss's story, I knew I would need some help beyond my own experience to get a few things right. Please forgive me if I took a few liberties in order to serve the purposes of my story.

Thanks to Coach (and dear friend) Carey Gallagher, for explaining the current scoring system for high school volleyball competition, and to Trent University varsity volleyball star (and my neighbour) Alex Campagnolo, for explaining cool moves that would make Anderson's skills as a setter stand out.

Math is not my domain, so I turned to some experts for help finding and solving a suitable Grade 11 math problem that would show off Bliss's unique gift. Thanks to:

Tristan Mills (BSc Physics and Astronomy/English, University of Waterloo; MSc Physics and Astronomy, Western

University), Emily Pass (BSc Physics and Astronomy, University of Waterloo; PhD Candidate, Astronomy, Harvard University), and Jack Bangay (BSc, MSc Physics, University of Guelph; Math/Physics teacher in the International Baccalaureate Diploma program), for creating and proofing those few lines of an appropriate quadratic equation. I include all their credentials simply because they're family, and I'm so proud of them all.

This story started with my love of yarn and knitting, and I've spent many hours with my fellow yarn devotees, chatting about knitting and crocheting, shopping for supplies, exploring craft fairs, and just generally submerging myself in this culture. A shout-out to my crafty friends, all of whom have shared stories, tea, and yarn projects with me: Heather Wright, Andria Hodgson, Callie Watson, and Barb Bangay (with whom I am "CNE compatible," and who deserves a special nod for suggesting String Theory as the name for the Adair family's store).

A special thank-you to my niece Kate Bangay, knitter extraordinaire, who supplied some fun terminology, and one line of an unusually twisty knitting pattern, when I reached out for help in making Bliss's thoughts as knitting-quirky as possible. (Yes, Katie, you get a paragraph of your own.)

Knitters love to take existing patterns and tweak them. That's what happens with the pattern for Bliss's Knitting Cure Baby Blanket. I adapted it from a pattern that can be downloaded from the Lion Brand yarn website (Diagonal Comfort Blanket). Lion Brand, like many yarn manufacturers, provides free patterns for all levels of knitters, and is a valuable source of information and projects for knitters and crocheters.

After working with Kid Lit icon Peter Carver on my three previous novels at Red Deer Press, this is my first project with editor Beverley Brenna. Her thoughtful, careful, and encouraging approach to editing reassured me from the start that Bliss and I were in good hands. Thank you, Bev!

Thanks also to copyeditor Penny Hozy, who has a gift for making writers look perfect on paper.

Writing is a solitary activity. As I travel further in this writing life, I am reminded over and over that I'm not alone out here, but rather, I'm part of a supportive and welcoming team. This book was written during the pandemic—for me, it was a period of isolation and anxiety—but my friends in the Canadian children's writing community were always there with support on social media and in person (okay, on Zoom), which made all the difference. A big thank-you to my CANSCAIP colleagues, and a special shout-out to Heather Wright and Lorna Schultz Nicholson for their much-appreciated writerly chats.

As always, thanks to my wonderful family. (It's okay, Tristan. I can't watch you on stage, so we're even ...) None of this writing adventure would matter if I didn't have them near, cheering me on.

INTERVIEW WITH JEAN MILLS

Sixteen-year-old Bliss Adair is a dedicated and successful knitter. Her parents run String Theory, a knitting shop in their small Ontario community. She has friends who knit. They're part of a Knitting Club that's preparing for an annual Clubs Bazaar at their high school. How did knitting come to be such an important element of this story?

I am a knitter, so using knitting as a framework for this story started with my own love for this craft. Holding knitting needles and yarn in my hands is definitely my happy place. I liked the idea of giving my main character her own happy place, an escape from the challenges she faces in dealing with her friends and their problems. But the technical side of knitting—patterns, complicated stitches, all the things that go wrong and need "the Help Desk"—mirrors Bliss's relationships with her friends, too. It's such a traditional craft, but it is surprisingly complex. Knitting is also trending right now, with lots of social media presence. Knitting is cool!

The first rule of knitting, as explained to Bliss by her mother, many years ago, is not to look too far ahead. Why is this important in knitting? How did you begin to envision this rule as a motif for this story, something that comes up again and again, as Bliss works on applying it to life as well as knitting?

There's an old Yiddish saying: *We plan, God laughs.* In other words, you can plan and organize your life all you want, but you never know what's coming. Everything can change in an instant. I don't knit anything complicated—I'm definitely not at Bliss's level—but even simple patterns require a lot of attention. I've learned that looking ahead on a pattern is pointless; those instructions in row 50 make no sense if you haven't completed rows 1–49. Life is like that, too, so following a knitting pattern is a perfect way to show how Bliss navigates the unexpected challenges she and her friends face in this story.

As a writer, you are known for realistic stories that invite readers to figure things out as we go along. Is this stance of not giving too much away at first, not spoon-

feeding your audience, related, somehow, to the first rule of knitting?

It's absolutely related to my appreciation for "the first rule of knitting!" I believe readers don't get enough credit. We have to work at understanding the many twists and turns of our lives, so why can't we, as readers, do the same thing? I love to play with plot structure and language, knowing my readers will be rewarded by working a little to navigate the story. Also, on a technical note, I love messing with sentence structure, especially since I always write in first person, in the voice of my main character. I don't believe we think in simple, well-organized sentences, so I like to get inside my characters' heads and create complicated sentences that unfold the way their thoughts do. Do readers have to work a bit to follow these unusual sentences? They do. As a creative writer, this makes me very happy and, I hope, brings my readers enjoyment, too.

As for The First Rule of Knitting, there is nothing more satisfying than getting past a confusing section of a pattern and saying, "Oh! Now I see how this works!" Writing, reading, knitting—I love the connection here.

Mathematics is as important to Bliss as knitting. Is there a gap in the depiction of strong, contemporary women as math minded? Were you consciously attempting to

fill this gap as you wrote this story? And what steps did you take to make sure the quadratic equations included were accurate—are they accurate?

I honestly don't know if there's a gap in the depiction of women as "math-minded," which probably says more about my own reading preferences than anything else: I read mysteries, often with women sleuths, whose intellectual skills are never in doubt. So, no, I was not consciously trying to fill a gap. I've known many scientifically gifted, math-minded girls and women, and I loved portraying a girl who fits that description, too.

Fun Fact: the scene in which Bliss solves the math problem in class with such ease is based on something that happened to me in Grade 11. Our math teacher, Mr. Hill, set us an algebra problem. My friend Carla and I were collaborating, and I was dutifully working through the step-by-step solution. But it only took seconds for Carla to announce the answer. When Mr. Hill asked her how she knew, she shrugged and said, "Well, I just see it." Mr. Hill completely understood that we were in the presence of a unique math wiz—but he still asked her to write out the proof.

I did consult some math experts I know (you can read about them in the Acknowledgments), so I'm confident the quadratic equation is correct. And yes, that level of math is way over my head!

It's interesting that Sydney and the father of her baby met at a competitive curling event. Curling seems to be an underrepresented activity in books for young people—is this something you were aware of as you created this story? Are you an experienced curler? How do you think an author's previous experiences can assist the action as stories unfold?

First, yes, I believe an author's life experience can be a huge advantage in creating a story. In writing my first book, *Skating Over Thin Ice,* I used my own musical experience in my depiction of Imogen, the musical prodigy, who loses herself in her music, just as I have been known to do (although I am definitely not a prodigy!). And in *The Legend,* I used my experience on the media bench for Curling Canada as a source for Griffin's sports media adventures.

I couldn't resist including some curling content in this story. This sport has been part of my life since childhood and, for over ten years, I combined my love of curling and writing on the Media & Communications team at Curling Canada.

Curling is a sport that combines physical and mental skills, with an emphasis on sportsmanship and respect. You can start as a preschooler and play into your senior years, and there's room for all levels of ability and accessibility. The sport, with its unique culture, hasn't made its way into stories for kids, and

I'd love to change that. So, Sydney is a curler, and Bliss's dad learned to dance at the local curling club.

The high school Bliss attends is a welcome place for kids to be who they are, most of the time. Sydney, a newcomer, is soon to have a baby, and finds a supportive peer group with Bliss and her friends. Do you think contemporary high schools in Canada have always been this way? Or are like this now? Or does your book hope to show us a context schools might still aspire to?

My own experience, years ago as a teen, and more recently as the mother and teacher of teens, is reflected in Bliss's story: distinct friend groups, social dynamics, kids being nice, kids being not-so-nice. I don't think this has changed much overall. I remember a Sydney-like girl appearing at our school in Grade 12, and being immediately absorbed into a group of girls, where she found support and friendship, and it was no big deal. Both of my kids had gay friends and trans friends in high school, as well as friends from different ethnic and religious backgrounds. Again, none of this factored into their relationships. They were just friends in the classroom, sharing experiences on sports teams or in drama productions. And yet, a high school in a community near me is currently dealing with harassment and violence against gay and trans students.

I prefer to focus on the high school culture that I've seen at work in the many schools I've been associated with, personally and in my writing life: where teens are showing us all how to be tolerant and supportive. Adults could learn a lot from kids.

Bliss moves into new territory when she starts working on math problems with Finn, and she even says at one point, "Boys scare me a little." Sydney's relationship experience is complicated and painful; Bethany seems to be able to flit from one relationship to the next; and Anderson's experience is unique and hopeful. Why did you want to show these different approaches to romantic teen relationships?

First of all, if there is any experience in life that reflects the first rule of knitting, it's romantic relationships. They begin in different ways and follow uncharted territory, with no guarantee where they will end up. Emotions are deeply involved, and, especially in the teen world, there are peer and family pressures as well. Exploring romantic relationships is a fact of teen life, so of course I needed to include that in the story.

But I was more interested in the "help desk" side of Bliss's life. I didn't want "romance" to be the driving force behind the story, and I didn't want to delve into the dark side of relationships, either.

As a result, Sydney's experience of teen pregnancy is seen only from her perspective. Bethany's failed romance is quickly forgotten, and Anderson's budding relationship is both hopeful and restrained. When the girls are sitting around watching a movie, and lamenting that there are no nice boys, I had fun imagining them watching the movie series *To All the Boys I've Loved Before*, with its story of timid Lara Jean and her first boyfriend, the good-hearted Peter. That's the tone I was trying to achieve.

Bliss and Anderson also have a wonderful friendship—another important kind of relationship to champion. Anderson's size essentially becomes an emblem of his strength, his self-awareness, and his kindness, all keys to his character. He is comfortable in his own body, and his size is just one of many ways that he is remarkable. I love Anderson—in many ways, he is one of my favourite characters.

Bliss does appear to be moving into a relationship with Finn, but with the same gentle approach I've taken in all my books. In *Skating Over Thin Ice*, it was Imogen and Nathan, in *Larkin on the Shore*, it was Larkin and Will, and in *The Legend*, it was Griffin and Rosie. I hope Bliss and Finn's potential romance reflects that same uncertain exploration of what comes next in a teen relationship.

What books did you enjoy reading when you were Bliss's age? Are there some echoes of any of these books

in this story, as Bliss thinks about her own reality? What books do you enjoy reading now? How does your reading influence you?

I was an avid reader, so by Bliss's age, Madeleine L'Engle and Lucy Maud Montgomery were behind me, and I was deep into the Adult section of the library. At age 12, I read my older brother's copy of *Catcher in the Rye* by J.D. Salinger, and it changed my writing life, by showing me how far a teen narrator's voice could go. But even as a teen, I loved the classics, like Jane Austen and Charles Dickens. In high school, I discovered J.R.R. Tolkein's *Lord of the Rings*, which sparked my love of Medieval and Old Norse literature. It was all grist to the mill for me, the aspiring young writer.

Currently, I read for escape and entertainment, mostly mysteries. And, confession time, I read very little contemporary YA fiction, because I don't want any other author's or character's voice in my head when I'm writing my own stories. When I'm writing, the only voice I want to hear is my own narrator's.

What came first, as you wrote this book—the plot, or the theme, or the characters ...? Has this trajectory been a pattern with any of your other writing, or do you tend to write each manuscript the same way?

Bliss's story started with my lifelong love of the fibre arts. Her character was a natural progression from that creative world: a girl who knits, who sees patterns in things, who solves problems. There were so many possibilities for her to get into difficulties and struggle with "the first rule of knitting." The plot and other characters developed after Bliss had taken hold of my imagination.

But every story I write is different in terms of what came first.

For instance, *Skating Over Thin Ice* started with a tiny idea about a famous kid (maybe a movie star?) showing up in a classroom, and the struggle to balance fame and friendship. *Larkin on the Shore* started years ago with a vague idea of a character who cries when she reads books. And *The Legend* was sparked by two things: my own experiences on the media bench, and a moving moment of connection between a small boy and a hockey star that I saw on social media.

Ideas are always percolating in my imagination. I let them swim around for a while before I start to work on them actively. I have to see the beginning and the end of the story, and I have to hear my character's voice, before I even start writing. It's a daunting and exciting process.

Thank you, Jean, for your detailed, thoughtful responses about *Bliss Adair and The First Rule of Knitting* and your writing process!